Dreams

Shy Brooks

Copyright © 2013 by Shy Brooks

All rights reserved. This book or any portion thereof may not be reproduced or used in any manner whatsoever without the express written permission of the publisher except for the use of brief quotations in a book review.

Printed in the United States of America

First Printing, 2013

ISBN: 1491009837
ISBN-13: 978-1491009833

Email: shybrooks15@yahoo.com

In memory of Image.
Riding won't ever be the same without you.

Dedicated to my family, friends, and those who just love to dream and watch those dreams come true.

Table of Contents

Chapter 1: Dreams and Tests ~~~~~~~~~7

Chapter 2: Bad News ~~~~~~~~~~~~~21

Chapter 3: Picnic Nightmares ~~~~~~~31

Chapter 4: The Rooster ~~~~~~~~~~~37

Chapter 5: Shopping ~~~~~~~~~~~~~47

Chapter 6: The Party ~~~~~~~~~~~~58

Chapter 7: Unexpected Events ~~~~~~~69

Chapter 8: Secrets in Anchorage ~~~~~~~75

Chapter 9: You! ~~~~~~~~~~~~~~~~~~86

Chapter 10: Questions Left Unanswered ~89

Chapter 11: Destination Barrow ~~~~~~~~93

Chapter 12: Powerful ~~~~~~~~~~~~~~118

Chapter 13: Truth ~~~~~~~~~~~~~~~~129

Chapter 14: Historic Find ~~~~~~~~~~141

Chapter 15: Home Again ~~~~~~~~~~~160

Chapter 16: Glen Rose ~~~~~~~~~~~~176

Chapter 17: Nixie ~~~~~~~~~~~~~~~~189

Chapter 18: Through Camp Arrow ~~~~200

Chapter 19: Grilled Rabbit? ~~~~~~~~~208

Chapter 20: Soar'n ~~~~~~~~~~~~~~~~~~221

Chapter 21: Wishes ~~~~~~~~~~~~~~~~~232

Chapter 22: Either Peace or War~~~~~~~252

Chapter 23: Bionans ~~~~~~~~~~~~~~~~268

Acknowledgments ~~~~~~~~~~~~~~~~~~282

Chapter 1
Dreams and Tests

My name is Kieth Forjd.

I'm the kind of person that you would see walking down the street and think I'm just another normal teenager. But I'm anything but normal.

I've always known I was different. Ever since I was very little I would do something different then my other classmates, even my old friends thought I was a bit odd.

But my life, my upside down life, changed dramatically the year I went on a simple expedition trip to Alaska with my 'scientist of a father'.

Jumping into the story right there, where I met the person who would change my life, would be efficient. But to really understand my story I need to start a few months before Alaska, where this crazy roller coaster started.

It was 3031, in the month of May.

The night everything started I had a dream. I've always dreamed, more often then others I'm sure, but this one was different.

~It was raining hard, a girl with soaking brown hair and clothes was standing in the middle of a deserted dirt road with bushes and trees on either side. She fiddled around with the watch on her wrist.

"Hello?"

Lightning struck nearby, thunder boomed.

"I think I've found him," she said excitedly.

"Found who?" he answered, the man's voice was slow and slurred, like he had trouble forming words.

"The one who can he-" The girl screamed then collapsed into the mud. "Are you there? Fauna?"

A man came out of the bushes; he was in the shadows, so I couldn't make out his face. He went over to the girl and took off her watch.

"I'm sorry," he whispered "But Fauna is no longer available." he then threw the watch against a tree, destroying it. Lightning hit the tree behind the man, briefly lighting up his face.~

I woke up screaming so loudly I thought my head was going to explode, until I realized I was in my bedroom. Thunder boomed outside making me jump. I took a few deep breaths until I calmed myself down. It was only a dream.

I've had this dream exactly three times. But this time it was no dream; it was a nightmare. I tried to forget the nightmare, vanquish the images from my mind, but it didn't work. Every time I tried the images just further buried themselves into my photographic mind.

I caught myself shivering, not because it was cold, but because I knew the man's face. I'd known him all my life; the man in my nightmare had raised me; he was my father.

As I sat up, I realized my clothes were soaked to the bone with sweat; my head had begun to throb as I got out of bed to open the shades of my second story window. I had just enough time to glance out at the faint glow of the early morning traffic lights through the dying rain before going over to my dresser to grab some fresh clothes and hop in the shower.

After feeling refreshed, I sat down on the bed about to write in my journal, when I realized the bed was wet too.

"House!" I called into the silent air.

"Good morning, Mister Kieth, would you like for me to make you your chocolate milk?" asked the 'Homes Outstanding Useful System of Electronics' (most people knew her as House) in her pleasant computer voice. She did everything from make beds to advanced house cleaning, which did take care of a few of the chores I hated, though she did a bit too much sometimes.

"No, I'll get that myself, but you can change my sheets please."

"Of course."

I went downstairs and made myself some chocolate milk. While I drank it I wrote down what I saw in my dream into my journal, not like I could ever forget but Dad always insisted that I did, so it's become a habit.

After I wrote the last detail and put my glass in the dishwasher I shouted into the air again.

"Is Dad still in the lab, House?"

"Yes," she replied, "But I believe he is getting ready to come up."

I sighed, "He's been in there all night, hasn't he?"

"As a matter of fact he has-"

She was cut off... the elevator doors opened up and out stepped Dad, lab coat trailing behind him.

"Good you're up," he said as he saw me standing in the middle of the brightening kitchen.

"Have you eaten?"

I shook my head no. Dad continued on through the kitchen and sat down at the bar before he said, "Well then, tell House what you want, go get your shoes on, then get in the car. You can eat on the way."

"On the way to where?" I asked, confused.

Dad stopped what he was doing, and then turned around and glared at me with his brown eyes, his arms crossed, "Think," he said.

I thought; then it hit me. How could I, of all people, forget! "Oh yeah!" I exclaimed, a sheepish grin on my face. I dashed upstairs into my bedroom and grabbed my shoes. I then hopped down the stairs and to the elevator, trying to get the shoes on my feet.

With a final hop I entered the elevator where dad was waiting. "You didn't get anything to eat," he said as he ate a strip of bacon, must have had eggs too.

"I had chocolate milk, plus I'm not that hungry."

"Whatever, starve," he said as he pushed the only button this elevator had. It had an 'L' on it, which stood for Lab, or Lower Level. The doors closed and the elevator descended. I hated the elevator. It always felt like we were falling, and for one who doesn't like heights, it's not a fun feeling. I held onto the brass bar, though I knew that wouldn't stop me from falling.

A moment later we were in the lab. It was pretty much just an old house, but filled to the brim with high tech thingamajigs. Dad has told me what each and everyone does, and I still remember what everything does. It would take a whole day, maybe more, to explain it all to anyone.

Dad had also collected a bunch of older things from the older days, things from the 18,19, and 2000s. These things cost a fortune nowadays because they were almost extinct.

We walked through the antique infested hallways and out through the doors to where we kept the old Manual Driven Ford truck. It was blue with leather seats and it ran on electricity. This truck was a bit older than me. It was made in 3012, so 19 years ago.

"Wanna drive?" Dad asked, tossing me the keys.

I caught them. "No," I said tossing them back, "We have to drive over that bridge to get there. And you know I'm a chicken when it comes to heights."

"I just thought, with you being the only one of your friends to have a manual drivers permit, the only one with any permit, you would want to drive."

"I don't want anyone to think I'm a show off, having my permit at a young age and all."

Nowadays you get your permit at sixteen and have to wait till your 18 to get the actual license, except of course, on special occasions...

"Fine, have it your way," Dad said as he started the truck, the engine came to life with a roar. "You are aware that we live on a floating piece of cement right?" he said as he steered the truck down the road.

A shiver ran through my body and I held onto the seat a little tighter. "Don't remind me."

Soon we arrived at the dreaded bridge. As we drove onto it, I closed my eyes, and counted down the seconds that I knew it would take to get across it at the speed we were going. Once I was done counting I opened my eyes and was in shock to see we were still high up on the bridge.

I gave a little shriek and grabbed onto the seat for dear life as I saw how high up we were. I closed my eyes before the world started to spin.

"Dad!" I moaned; that only made him burst out laughing.

He was still chuckling as we walked into a room marked 'cerebral studies' in the building of the 'Top Secret Scientific Studies Lab' in Dallas. This was the 11th time I've walked through those doors. Dad has brought me to this place every year since he figured out I was 'different'. Even when we had lived in London he brought me here.

The place still looked the same, same old glass doors, same old tile floors. It almost looked like a hospital would have looked in the 2000s.

I came here to be tested for my cerebral intellect,

or in other words, I was the scientists' lab rat. This time would be a bit different, because somehow the Guinness World Record guys found out that I had existed and they wanted to dub me the 'most intelligent kid alive'. Apparently the 'top secret' part of the Top Secret Scientific Studies Lab wasn't strictly adhered to.

We walked up to the front desk and signed in. Then we walked through the door that Dad opened with a swipe of a card.

I took a deep breath before walking through the door that Dad held open for me. It went from ear splitting loudness to absolute silence in a matter of seconds. Multiple pairs of eyes followed me as I entered the room. I realized that my clothes were inappropriate for the occasion; I was wearing my outside messy clothes, while everyone else had suits and ties. Bad choice on my part.

I was glad when two of the scientists in pristine white lab coats came and escorted me into yet another room. There they gave me a set of special white, skintight clothes, kind of like what they used in motion capture films. It was designed to record all of my actions during the tests. When I put them on, the scientists came back in and helped me put on my 'swimming cap', as they called it, over my red hair. It was a bit tight, but they said that it had to get the sensors as close to my skin as possible. So now I looked like a mummy, everything covered except for my face, which they soon covered up with some clear glass glasses that would record what my eyes did during the tests, but I could still see.

When I came back out into the main room, I noticed the Guinness guys were sitting in the back corner of the large room. Now I felt embarrassed, wearing these vacuum tight clothes.

I headed over to a table that was in the front of the room. At the table occupying one of the two chairs was a middle-aged man with brown hair.

As I neared the table the man looked up at me from some paperwork he had been reading.

He said, "Ah, Mr. Forjd! Always a pleasure to meet you!"

"Likewise, Mr. Newark," I said as I shook his hand, "But please, just call me Kieth."

"Of course. Now let's get started. If you'd follow me please."

We walked over to where all the scientists were seated, my Dad being one of them. They all grew quiet as we stood in front of them.

"Good morning everyone!" Nexryt Newark said a bit too happily; there were some replies of 'good mornings' back.

He continued, "Now as you all may very well know this," he put his hand on my shoulder, "This is Kieth Forjd."

There was a chorus of 'hellos' and 'how are you's'. I've never been good in crowds but I replied in kind, "Morning."

Mr. Newark raised his hands for quite saying, "Now I want each of you to stand, state your name and where you're from, then sit back down, please. Let's start with you, Mr. Baxon."

Thus began the tests.

They had me do a multitude of things including very complicated math, without a calculator. Some of the scientists could not even do the math they made me do, while I had it all mastered at the age of five.

One of the scientists asked me a word problem, "How long does it take to get across the '50ft Tall Bridge' at the required speed?"

I glared at Dad, who was just behind the scientist who had asked me the question, then said, "Usually just one minute, unless the driver of the vehicle decides to slow down."

Everyone in the room burst out in laughter, someone was getting it when we got home...

After the math tests, they had me do what they called the 'Memory Maze'. Before hand they had me glance at a piece of paper that would tell me how to get out, I only had a second to look at it, but that was enough.

They then blindfolded me, and lead me to the start. It didn't take me long before I was out of the many twists and turns, ups and downs of the extravagant maze. And when I took off my blindfold the scientists were all standing there, dumbfounded.

The first to realize I was just standing around waiting for my next test was Mr. Newark. He came over to me, slapped me on the back, and said, "Congratulations, you just beat the record for the Memory Maze! And that's saying something, considering the previous record holder had months to memorize the way through and was not blindfolded."

At the end of the day, I had my picture taken by the Guinness Record guys, thankfully in my regular clothes, and then they gave me a plaque that said that I was the most intelligent kid alive.

After many congratulations we finally managed to get outside and into the truck. The sun was just setting in the orange sky.

On the way back to the house I replayed, in my mind, all that had happened today. I had a tendency to do this when I didn't have anything else to do. It seemed to help me find details that I had missed earlier; for example, I realized Dads hair had been wet when he came inside the house that morning.

I inquired this of Dad. He simply replied, "Someone has to feed the dog that's been hanging around the lab."

When we arrived at the lab it was too dark to see, so Dad flicked on the light switch.

"That dog, by the way, turned out to be very sweet. So I had House put her up in your room. She's yours if you want her," he said as we entered the elevator.

I thought Dad had lost his mind, "My own dog?" I said, a little excited, Dad had never been a big fan of animals.

My excitement faded as I remembered the reasons he had given me things before.

"What's the catch?" I cautiously asked.

"Oh, there's no catch." we walked into the kitchen. "Just don't name it Bobo," he mumbled.

"Yes there is; there's always a catch," I whispered, "Where are we going this time?"

Dad sighed, and then confessed, "Alaska, we are going to Alaska."

I felt angry at the thought of having to go so far away.

"Alaska!" I burst out, "How long?"

"I don't know, two months maybe longer, depending on-"

I cut him off, knowing too well what he was saying, "Depending on what we find, I know, I know."

I sat down on the bottom step of the stairway; Dad joined me.

"Kieth, I know you don't like going on these expeditions, but I'm sure this time, we'll find what we are looking for-"

I stood and yelled at Dad, "That's what you said last time!"

I was angry now. The first time we had this conversation was in London, where we used to live. I was just glad we still had our home in Texas, though we seemed to travel at least once a year to some remote location for some expedition related to his love for science.

"I don't want to move again! I have friends here. I don't want to leave them."

Actually, if truth be told, I only had one friend. Her name was Kit, but I sometimes call her Kitty Kat. I liked Kitty because I could be myself around her and not feel stupid for being too smart.

He looked at me, then said, "What if I made a deal with you?"

I crossed my arms, "It all depends on the deal being made."

"What if I promise that we won't move again no matter what happens?"

I looked into his eyes for a moment; he wasn't lying. But I didn't want to answer.

"How bout I let you sleep on it; you've had a long day."

"Agreed," I yawned, I hadn't realized it until just then, but I was tired.

Dad stood, "All right then, get off to bed, and give that dog a name."

I grabbed a couple pieces of chicken from the fridge before I headed upstairs to my bedroom. And as I entered, sure enough, I saw, there lying on my bed, a snow-white dog, and the very exact dog that had been hanging around the town for months now.

The dog made no movement as I walked over to the desk to put my World Guinness Record Plaque down.

The dog was facing me; she had her eyes closed. So I sat down, cross-legged, on the floor with one of the pieces of chicken in my hand and held it out to the dog. I clucked my tongue. The dog made no response. I snapped my fingers. Still no response. After a few minutes of trying, I gave up and decided to change into my pj's, and then I tried again.

Finally believing the dog to be deaf, I sat back on my hands and closed my eyes. When I looked up again, I was surprised to find that the dog was staring at me with bright green eyes. I held out the chicken again.

"Want some?" I asked, as I slowly crawled up to the dog, her eyes glued on to me. I got within an arms length before she lifted her head and sniffed the air.

"Smells good, doesn't it?" I then set my hand, full of chicken, down on the bed, palm up. She slowly approached the food. I let out a sigh as she finally got up and licked the chicken off my hands.

"There ya go." I gently rubbed behind her ear. There seemed to be an instant connection between us, I had this weird feeling like we had met before.

"Now," I asked the dog, "how bout you get off my bed so we can both go to sleep?"

Almost as if she understood me, she hopped off the bed. With her great big head and feet, kind eyes and fluffy white fur I could only assume she was a Great Pyrenees. Now very, very tired, I tore back the covers and got into bed.

I patted the bed. "You can sleep up here if you like." She took the invitation and took a spot near my feet. The lights automatically went off as I tried to think of a name for the dog.

As soon as I started thinking about it a name came into my head "Blanket!" I sat up, confused, the name was so familiar, yet I knew no one by that name. "Snow Blanket, it fits." She licked my cheek then snuggled my feet again. I lay back down still confused, and fell into an uneasy sleep.

Chapter 2
Bad News

I had another dream that night.

~It was dark out but I could see the outline of an old town, one that seemed to be falling apart, abandoned long ago, though not quite empty. The scene changed. A door, then a dark room with a bed that had the faint out line of a~

I jumped up, opening my eyes. Something was in front of my face. I sighed, realizing it was Blanket then glanced at the clock, another early morning. I sighed, rubbing my temples as I realized my head hurt. Why did it always hurt after a dream? No one knew of the headaches other than me, not even Dad, I didn't want to worry him. I wrote down what I saw into my dream journal. I noticed Blanket staring at me as I wrote the last sentence.

I got up to go get dressed but as soon as I stood my vision went fuzzy, and the pain in my head peaked to where it was almost unbearable. The floor rushed up to meet me. It was over almost as quickly as it had started. But I still lay on the floor, hands clutching my throbbing head; I was too shocked to move.

Blanket came over and started to lick my hands, only then did I dare sit up, removing my hands from my face.

Sloppy wet kisses then bombarded me, "Eew,

stop, stop!" I pushed her away playfully. As I got up, she looked at me with curiosity. "Don't worry, I'm fine." I slowly walked into the bathroom so I could wash off the 'kisses'.

It was 8:30 when I arrived in the kitchen for breakfast, Blanket on my heels. I already ordered cereal and chocolate milk from House, who insisted she would get it for me, and was already halfway done with it when Dad arrived from the lab.

"Good morning!" he said cheerfully. "Have you thought about my offer?"

Avoiding the answer I said, "Why does it seem like your bedroom is now in the lab? It like you just live in there now."

He just chuckled, then ordered his breakfast. "Now" he said, sitting down, "What about my offer?"

I hesitated, I was scared of what he might say, "Cross your heart we won't move?"

"Cross my heart," he answered.

We were both silent for a few moments as we ate. Our silence was shortly broken by a whimper from Blanket. She was looking up at me with big sad doggie eyes.

"So," Dad said, noticing Blanket for the first time, "What did you name our new family member?"

"Dad, this is Blanket. Blanket, this is my Dad." Dad bent down to pet her. But as he reached out to her, Blanket ran off and hid behind the counter.

"That's odd," I noted, "She hasn't done that with

me." I asked House if she could make something for Blanket. One minute later she was eating a bowl of mixed meats that House had made for her. I sat down on the floor next to Blanket, patting her on the back, thinking.

As Dad sat at the bar, looking through some kind of paperwork, a sudden thought occurred to me.

"When are we leaving for Alaska?" I asked.

He glanced at me, "Middle or late July."

I continued to pet Blanket until she finished her food, then I stood, went up to my room, and sat down on the bed. I had nothing to do.

July, I only have two months! I lie down on the bed and let out a long sigh. Why, after years of living in Texas, did he have to choose now to leave!

I needed to talk to someone, so I picked up my cell phone and texted Kit.

'R u doing anything?' I wrote 'I need to talk w- you.'

Only a moment passed before she replied. 'only school... can it wait?'

'no not really, it's important. cant you ask your mom for the day off?' I asked.

Kit and her two siblings were homeschooled. I was asking her for a lot, but I really needed to talk to someone.

'she wants to know what's so important that her daughter can't finish school.'

I replied by saying, 'what if u bring your school to 'The Place' and I can help you with it while we talk?'

'sounds ok, meet you in the stables in 20?'

'k, say thnx to ur mom for me.'

Kit and her family had horses, so we would be riding to their 'fort' to go talk. I put on my riding jeans and boots then ran downstairs, Blanket at my heels. Dad was still in the kitchen doing paperwork.

"I'm gonna go riding with Kit. So I'll see you later, okay?"

He didn't even look up from his work as he said, "Fine, be careful."

I was almost in the elevator when I decided to grab some sandwich type stuff to bring along.

It took me only fifteen minutes to ride my bike to her house, which was in Alvord. I loved the fresh air that was here, out of the way of the upper cities. As I approached her house I had to get off my bike to open the gate then carefully walk over the cattle guard. Blanket, who had followed me, went through the barbed wire. I got back on and went up the driveway towards the stables.

When I got there she was already brushing off the horses. I parked the bike against a fence post then walked over to her.

"Hey," she said as she heard me trying to sneak up behind her.

"Howdy." I replied in a Texas accent I didn't have. Although I was a Texan by birth, I had spent my younger years living in London.

"I've already brushed Cowboy off for you." she said indicating the blackish brown gelding that was tied up to the stall. "His saddle's already out."

"Thanks," I went over to put on his saddle blanket.

I was about to put the bit in his mouth when Kit asked "Is that the dog that's been hanging around your place?"

"Yeah, that's the one. Dad gave her to me; I named her Blanket."

"Cool," she said. She was already on her horse, Image who was a beautiful paint with one blue and one brown eye, while I was still struggling to put the bit in Cowboy's mouth.

After the bit was in his mouth I put the sandwich stuff in my saddlebags, and hoisted myself into the saddle.

"Ready?" Kit asked as I clumsily put my feet into the stirrups.

"Yup." We trotted off down the familiar path that led to the trails.

Kit was an excellent rider. She and her horse Image competed in endurance races, so they both had to be fit. Not many people knew about the connection they shared. I never could explain it but they seemed to always know what the other was thinking. My Dad had actually been involved in the process, that's how we met. We became friends quickly, understanding each other, and soon shared a love for riding horses.

"So," Kit said as we found the special trail that lead to the fort. "What's bothering you?"

I fiddled around with the reins, "I'd rather not say

right now. Let's wait till we get to The Fort."

She stared at me then said, "Alrighty then," she laughed, "Race ya there!"

As soon as she said it, Image set off at a lope, running far up ahead of Cowboy and me. It didn't take long though for us to catch up.

We were forced to slow down as we neared The Fort, which had a bunch of bushes around it. The fort was a very old 18th century log cabin. Most of it had fallen apart, but we had fixed some of it up. We dismounted the horses and put them in the makeshift corral. I took the bread and peanut butter out of my saddlebags.

Kit grabbed her schoolwork from Image's saddlebags and set her stuff on the porch of the house, I started making her a sandwich. I knew exactly how she liked it. I finished and handed it to her, then made my own. In a moment, I sat down on the aged wood of The Fort's porch, alongside Kit, and started eating my sandwich.

It was a beautiful day. There was a slight breeze blowing through the greening trees that surrounded the Fort. There was also a patch of dandelions near the corral where the two horses stood grazing the fresh green grass.

"I wish things didn't have to change," I blurted out before I could stop it.

"What do you mean by change? Things change everyday," she said. When I didn't reply she took my hands, looked into my eyes and asked, "What's wrong Kieth; can't you tell me now?"

I looked away; I didn't want to have to give her, what I considered to be the worst news ever. I hated making people sad, "Kitty I don't know how to tell you this but..." I hesitated not wanting to continue.

"But what?" she urged. I sighed, and then told her straight out what had been bothering me since last night. "We're going to Alaska."

She was silent, I dared not look at her, but she was silent so long, I eventually had to glance at her.

I knew it, she looked so sad. It took a while, but finally she said, "How long?"

"I don't know, a year, two even. Thinking about how his last big expedition turned out, we could possibly move there, though he promised me we wouldn't."

"When do you leave?"

"Middle, or late July."

She seemed to relax a little, "Well, at least I'll be able to give you a *big* 15th birthday party!"

I was shocked; I'd never had a 'big' party before. "You don't have to do that."

"Yes I do!" she snapped at me, "I'm your friend, and that's what a best friend does. Should've done it years ago..." she mumbled on.

"That's real sweet of you, but who are you going to invite, you're my only real friend."

"Well it would be me, you, my family, and your dad of course!" she said happily.

I sighed, "Okay, I guess I'll agree to come then."

"You'll have to come, it's your party after all." She laughed.

We then sat in silence, merely enjoying each other's company, as we finished the last of bites our sandwiches.

Blanket, who had been lying by the corral, watched me with deep intelligent eyes. It was a little creepy by just how intelligent they looked. It was almost as if she had understood every one of our words. After a moment of looking into those odd eyes, I called her over.

"Here Blanket have the rest of my sandwich." She did just that. She came over and devoured what was left.

"Your a hungry dog," Kit noted.

"Yeah she is, I had House make her something this morning. But who knows how long she's been without food." I stared at Blanket for a moment longer, when all of a sudden something hit me.

"Ouch!" I protested, rubbing the back of my head. "What'd you do that for?" I looked at Kit who had her thick Physical Science book in her hands and a wry smile on her face.

"You had a big bug on your head, and I was just trying to get it off," she lied, "It was this big." She spread her arms out wide demonstrating.

"If there was a big bug on my head you should have used your hands not your Science book! Anyway I'm pretty sure I would have felt a bug that big," I gave her a little laugh, happy for the first time that day.

"Now," I said, the weight of Alaska off my shoulders, "Let's get to your school."

"Fine, Professor Forjd." she joked.

I tensed, "I've told you not to call me that!" The kids at school used to call me that, and I didn't like it.

"I'm sorry, it's just you've already graduated, and even taught at college. I wish I could do that!"

"You know it wasn't my choice to teach, and Dad told me I should just get college over with, so I did." I remembered the days at the university, being only nine years old when I graduated, one of the youngest yet.

"So what module are you on?" I asked, trying changing the subject to her Physical Science.

"Module ten," she said, flipping to the chapter.

"Aw, Newton's Laws." I had already read her book, and knew what was where, so I asked her some questions regarding the chapter.

"What is Newton's second law?"

"My way of remembering it, or yours?" she asked.

"Your way."

She smiled as she said, "May the mass times acceleration be with you."

I laughed, "And how does that help you remember Newton's second law?"

"Well, its obvious isn't it?" It wasn't obvious so I shook my head no; she continued, "Mass times acceleration equals total force."

I gave her a blank stare and when I still didn't get it she said, "Force! Kieth, force! May the force be with you!"

"Oh, Star Wars, that's an old movie! It's like a thousand years old!"

We both laughed. Then laughed some more as the subjected strayed far from Newton's laws of motion. We sat for hours just talking until finally I needed to go home.

Chapter 3
Picnic Nightmares

I did many things in the months leading up to my birthday. I tried to teach Blanket tricks and it seemed like it only took her a few tries to learn it. It almost seemed as if she was trying to give me the satisfaction of actually teaching her something even though she seemed to already know how to do it. But time flew by quickly, and despite the fact that I really didn't want a party, I starting looking forward to it. Kit's constant questions about what I wanted and didn't want to do were starting to excite me.

It was Friday, July the second, two weeks before Dad and I would leave on the sixteenth and two days before my birthday on the fifth. Kit had decided that instead of celebrating my birthday on Monday we would celebrate it on the Fourth so she could add fireworks to the celebration. By now I just agreed to anything she wanted to do.

Right now Kit and I had ridden to The Fort for a picnic. We lay down on the grass, bellies full, and watched the fluffy white clouds pass overhead. Kit was talking to me about the different types of clouds that she saw, but I wasn't really listening.

My thoughts were on the dream I kept having. About the old town in the dark, and most of all, the room with the bed. The dream had been the same since I had first had it two months ago and it always ended in the same spot. It was beginning to annoy me, almost to the point where I didn't want to sleep at night because I would have the same exact dream and the same headache. The headaches were lasting longer than usual now, sometimes all day.

Today was one of those days. I tried closing my eyes to soothe the pain but it didn't help.

Suddenly I was in the old building again, but this time was different, Dad was there. He said something but I couldn't understand him. He walked off. Instead of following him I went down another hallway into the room with the bed. I walked over to it took off the covers and saw a-

I woke with a jolt. Kit was shaking me.

"You scared me!" she said, releasing me. "I said your name, like a million times, and you wouldn't wake up!"

It took me a moment to come to my senses. Once I did, I didn't like what I felt. Sitting up I put my throbbing head between my knees and wrapped my arms around my legs. I felt Kit put a hand on my back.

I hardly heard her say, "Kieth? Are you okay?"

It took a moment before the pain lessened then I looked up at her and nodded. I lay back down, exhausted. Kit sat crisscrossed next to me, watching me closely with her hazel eyes.

"Are you sure?" she asked.

I nodded again, not trusting my voice to speak properly. Kit felt my forehead.

"You're sweating," she said.

I just closed my eyes, her cool hand felt good

upon my seething forehead. I then took her hands and pressed them against my head sighing as the pain lessened even more.

"Kieth, didn't you hear me? Your forehead is sweaty."

"Sorry," I released her hands from my grip. I saw her wiping sweat off on her jeans.

"You sure your not sick?" she asked.

"Yes, I'm sure. I'm just tired." I stood.

"Tired from what? You just had a nap, the only reason I woke you was because you were moaning."

"Tired of my dreams." I walked over to the porch where Blanket lay.

She had been mad at me when the heat of summer kicked in because I shaved her. But now that her white coat was growing back in she was a little happier. I sat next to her and petted the soft fur on her face.

Kit came over and sat on the other side of Blanket. "Tell me about it," she said. "About what?" I knew perfectly well what, and she told me so. "Fine, fine!" I interrupted her ranting. "I'll tell you."

I'd never told anyone of these strange dreams, just wrote them down and tried to forget them. Though this time, I told her everything, figuring if there was anyone I could trust about this, it would be her.

"Just lately," I finished, a few minutes later, "My head has been hurting longer and also more intense than usual. I don't know what's wrong, it just does that, and it has for a very long time."

"Why haven't you told me about this before?" she asked.

"I figured you'd think I was crazy, having weird dreams and all," I answered.

Kit laughed, startling Blanket, who had fallen asleep.

"Me, think you, crazy? I'm connected to a horse in a way that not even the scientist who actually created the serum can understand and you think your dreams are crazy?"

I guess I should have known better than to think she'd view me as weird for something like this.

"I still think I'm going crazy, though," I said.

"We're all crazy in our own weird way, Kieth."

"Yeah, I guess you're right," I agreed.

We both sat in silence for a few moments, enjoying the day. In those few moments I thought of what I had seen and if it really meant anything. I was very confused and I hated being confused about something.

Usually I could just recall something of my past to help the confusion but I got nothing when I went back and thought about it. My dreams had always confused me.

"Oh my!" Kit exclaimed, bringing me back to reality.

"What?" I asked, startled.

She stood up, looking at her phone, "We have to get back to the house!"

I stood too, "Why?"

"I thought you had an 'internal clock' in your

head! And didn't I tell you to remind me that we needed be back at four! " She said running over to the corral.

She had told me that, I felt bad now. "I'm sorry I-"

"Don't tell me you forgot!" she snapped.

"That's not what I was going to say, I had a lot on my mind, that's all."

She just rolled her eyes.

"We have to go!" she started to tighten Images saddle up.

"Why?" I asked again, starting to tighten Cowboys saddle too, I didn't want to be left alone if she took off.

"We have to be home for dinner or my mom is gonna yell at us!" she answered as she threw herself onto Image's back.

"But why is it so important that we have to hurry!" I said hopping onto Cowboy.

She smiled a secretive smile, "You'll see once we get there!"

Before I could ask anything else, she loped off in the direction of her house.

I sighed, girls and their many secrets.

"Come on Blanket!" I called but there was no need, for she was already at my side. I gave Cowboy the signal to go and soon enough we were loping a short distance behind Image and Kit.

It took us only a few minutes to get back to the house and soon I figured out why Kit wanted to hurry. Her Grandparents were coming to visit for the weekend.

Chapter 4
The Rooster

"Kieth!" Kit said hurriedly. "Get two eggs out for these brownies!"

"On it!" I answered sliding over to the silver fridge on the freshly swept wood floor.

The moment we had the horses up, Kit's mom put us to work immediately.

Her grandparents had just landed in Dallas and would be at the house in half an hour or so.

Right now we were on brownie making duty. Kit's grandparents loved to have her homemade brownies when they were visiting.

I opened up the huge double doors of the fridge and searched its interior for an egg.

"There's only one!" I finally said after double searching the fridge.

"Darn! Go get another from the coop then!" she was already mixing the oil with the brownie mix.

I dashed out the back door and almost ran over Kit's younger brother, Troy, who was sweeping off the porch.

"Sorry." I said slipping on my boots real quick, then continuing to the coop.

Once there I grabbed the well-used trash can lid, that had a handle on it, and placed this in front of me like a shield. Only then did I enter the coop. I kept an eye out for the rooster, the main reason I had the shield. The rooster was awfully mean and very protective of his hens.

I was able to reach the hens' nests without any sign of him. So I grabbed the greenish colored eggs that were lying in the fresh hay and stuck them in a pouch I had made with my shirt; I had forgotten to grab the basket.

I grabbed the last egg, still no sign of the rooster, or any chicken for that matter, they must've all be scratching around for whatever little bugs they could find outside.

I turned towards the exit. My shoulders slumped. "Oh just my luck!"

There standing in the only way out was the rooster. His hens were filed behind him; it must be roosting time.

The rooster stopped in the doorway and stared at me. As far as the rooster knew I was some kind of egg thief. We stared each other down, sizing the other up. I held up my makeshift shield and tightened my grip on my shirt that was weighed down with eggs.

Slowly I walked towards the rooster knowing that at any moment he could attack me. I managed to get right up to the rooster before it made its move. The rooster ran at me, aiming for my legs. I tried to jump over the rampaging rooster. Dropping several eggs in the process, yolks broke out of their shells.

I made it to the doorway, in between the rooster and his hens. A very bad place to be. He ran at me again this time it had more speed so it actually jumped at me. I couldn't run away from the evil little rooster so I held up the trash can lid against his attack. But I misjudged the rooster's flight, I thought it was going for my midsection, but instead it flew a little higher.

"Ouch!" I yelled.

The rooster had aimed for my head and was now attacking my face. I let go of the shield and fell to the ground then reached out for the rooster's legs, I let go of my shirt in the process and all the eggs were either crushed or cracked on the ground.

I wrestled with the rooster for a moment before I finally managed to grab both of its legs.

"Gotcha!" I stood then tossed the rooster in the coop with the rest of his hens and slammed the door on it before it could reach the ground.

I sighed, how could I be so stupid! All I needed was one egg, if I hadn't decided to get them all could I have avoided that little fight.

I looked at my shirt. It was covered in egg yolks. I smiled as I looked around at the remains of the eggs; there was still one whole egg. I picked it up and headed back to the house.

When I arrived at the porch Troy was gone, probably doing another chore.

I took off my boots before entering then slowly walked into the kitchen. Kit was making some lemonade now.

"I got the egg," I said quietly coming up behind her.

"Good, put it in the batter please." she never looked up from her measuring of the lemonade mix.

I did what she said; I was already mixing it in when she asked, "What took you so long?"

She was right behind me now so all I had to do was turn around for her to get the story. First her face was that of shock, and then she was fighting to keep back a smile.

"Oh, my," she said trying not to laugh. Her eyes narrowed as she looked at my face.

"You have a cut on your forehead."

I hadn't noticed before, but my forehead was stinging slightly. I was about to reach up to see how bad it was but Kit caught my hand before it could even get near it.

"Nah-ah" she said, "Your hands are filthy, and so is your shirt. Let me patch up your head then you can go get one of Troy's shirts. So come here and sit down and I'll go get the first aid kit."

She shoved me onto a stool while she went into the pantry to get the first aid kit.

While she was in there searching for it her sister, Tezibell, came from the hallway, which led to her room. She gasped as she saw me sitting there on the stool. Must look worse than I thought.

"Oh my!" she said, "What happened to you?"

I gave her a small chuckle, "Your evil little rooster."

She came closer to me, "Oh he scratched you!"

"I'm quite aware of that; Kit is getting the first aid."

Tezibell walked over to the sink and grabbed a handful of paper towels.

"Here." she handed them all to me, I stuck it on my forehead; it stung a bit as I touched the cut.

"Tez?" Kit called from the pantry, "Do you know where the first aid kit is?"

"Last time I saw it was on the top shelf" she called back.

I heard the screech of a stool then Kit said, "Got it!" she came back into the kitchen with the distinctive red box in her hand.

"Tezibell, go wash your hands then you can help me."

"Help you! It can't be that bad can it?" I asked.

She took out her phone and pulled up her camera app. I looked at myself first it was my face and a bloody towel then when I moved the towel I saw that the rooster had given me three long scratches across my forehead.

"Oh, you'll need help. And a lot of band aids" I added.

They made me lay on the floor so they could work on me better. First they cleaned the wound.

They kept telling me how lucky I was that it wasn't deeper or else I would've had to get stitches.

They also kidded me that they were going to put girly band- aids on my head. At least I hoped they were kidding.

In the middle of it all Troy walked in and asked us just what we were doing.

"We're fixing Kieth's head," answered Tezibell, "He was attacked by the rooster."

"Troy," Kit said, she was putting on the third

band-aid "Could you stick the brownies in the oven? Then after you do that go get Kieth one of your shirts."

I heard Troy as he put the batter in the oven then head off to his room.

"All right, that's the last one." Kit said as Troy came back with a T-shirt.

I stood, they finally allowed me to touch my head, I felt the band-aids all across it. "Oh joy, I bet I look lovely."

We all started laughing. Just then Kit's mother and father came into the room. Her mother had been dusting and her father just finished vacuuming. Kit's family didn't have a House system.

"What's so funny?" asked Mrs. Friesian. Then she caught sight of my head. "Oh my, Kieth, what happened to you?"

"The rooster." I replied. She rolled her eyes.

"We do need to do something about him, don't we?"

I just smiled. Kit's mother was always joking.

"Yes, you do."

"How did he manage to get you though?" asked Mr. Friesian.

"Yes, I'd like to know that too. I'd also like to know why you're covered in egg yolks," exclaimed Kit.

So I started to tell them all how I tried to get all the eggs and how the rooster had cornered me but I was interrupted by a soft beeping noise that came from the living room.

"They're here!" said Tezibell, leaping for the door.

The rest of her family quickly followed her. I hung back; Troy had left the clean shirt on the counter so I went to the bathroom to change. Once clean I came back into the kitchen where Mr. Friesian was bringing in some luggage.

"Need help?" I offered.

"No need Kieth, I got it. But there's some more outside in the car."

I headed outside to where the car was, as soon as I stepped out the door Blanket joined me.

"Where ya been, girl?" I asked.

We both continued walking to where Kit, and the rest of her family were gathered; they were all exchanging hugs. I didn't want to bother them so I went to the back of the car to where the rest of the luggage was. I grabbed a backpack and two suitcases and started to head back to the house.

"There you are Kieth!" I was forced to stop at the sound of Kit's voice. She came over to me and took the suitcases out of my grip.

"Don't be shy, come say hi!" She dragged me over to where her grandparents were; they were talking to Mrs. Friesian.

"Grandma, you remember Kieth?" Kit said enthusiastically pushing me closer to her.

Her grandma looked at me, a smile came upon her kind face. "Of course I remember Kieth, the smart kid."

She gave me a hug. "Oh dear, what happen to

your head?" she said releasing me.

"Let's just say, I learned not to get between a rooster and his hens," I said.

"Speaking of chickens," said Mrs. Friesian, "Dinner is hot and ready so let's get out of this heat and go inside to eat."

We all ended up carrying a bag of some sort, all I was left with was the backpack I'd slung onto my back.

Once we all were back inside we dropped off our burdens into Kit's room, where her grandparents would be staying for the week.

Everyone then became busy in the kitchen. Kit went to tend her brownies with her grandma. Her mother was cutting up the moist chicken and Troy and Tezibell were setting the table while I was helping Kit's dad and grandpa fill cups with ice.

I have always liked hanging out with Kit and her family because it was so different from my own. All I had was Dad, which was never as interesting as this family was.

As I filled the last glass with ice and was about to sit down at the table I realized it was six o'clock. Dad might be worried if I didn't get home soon. So I went over to where Kit was cutting her brownies into perfect squares.

"Hey, I gotta head home," I said to her.

She paused in her brownie cutting. "Right now?" she asked. "We're about to eat."

"Yeah right now." I sighed, "I don't want to worry my dad."

"Why don't you just call him?"

"He's in the lab."

"Oh." Kit knew that my dad never answered the phone while he was in the lab.

"Well at least take a doggie bag home." she said, finishing the last cut on her brownies. She took the knife and fished a slice out of the pan and wrapped it in foil then handed it to me.

"Here's your dessert." She smiled.

"Why thank you." I smiled back.

"Now, now," said Kit's grandma, "No dessert before dinner."

"Kieth's going home," Kit explained.

"So early?"

I nodded. Mrs. Friesian joined the conversation.

"I really wish you'd stay Kieth, we have plenty of food and you know you're always welcome here."

"I know, and thank you but I really must be headed home," I said, although I really wanted to accept her offer.

"I told him we'd give him a doggie bag," Kit said.

"Good idea," said Mrs. Friesian before she went to get me some chicken.

"You will come back tomorrow won't you?" asked Kit, "Grandma is taking us to Upper Decatur to go shopping. I'm sure she wouldn't mind if you tagged along. Would you Grandma?"

"Of course I don't mind!" she said happily, "The more the merrier!"

"Soooo," Kit gave me the doggie eye look, "Will you go with us?"

Taking the doggy bag from Mrs. Friesian, I said, "Um, I will have to ask my dad first, but I'm sure it will be fine with him."

"Great!" she said "See ya tomorrow then."

"Well," I chuckled, walking towards the door, "If you insist on me coming, you might as well use our house as an entrance to the city, you can even use our car."

"Foods getting cold," Troy complained playfully.

"All right, all right. I'm leaving." I opened the door seeing the sun low in the sky. It wasn't dark yet, but the positioning of the Upper city made it darker then it should be right before the sun set.

"Bye guys," I said, Blanket joined me, "See y'all tomorrow."

Everyone said bye back before I shut the door. Then I got onto my bike and rode down the gravel driveway, Blanket trotting along not far behind.

Chapter 5
Shopping

Fifteen minutes later I arrived home, parked my bike outside, and was now sitting in the kitchen eating dinner. Dad had been in the lab, as he always was, and only when I asked if I could go shopping with the Friesians did he say anything. He only said one syllable 'yes'. That was enough for me though.

I tried to finish what I could of the moist chicken, but ended up giving Blanket most of it. My head had begun to throb again.

"House," I called as I climbed the flight of stairs to my room.

"Yes?" she answered.

"If Dad asks, tell him I've gone to bed." I was already in my room, putting on my PJs.

"Of course, is there anything else you need Mister Kieth?"

I was about to answer 'no' but as I got into bed got into bed I answered instead, "Yeah, text Kit and tell her I'm coming with them tomorrow."

"Done," she said immediately.

Satisfied, I pulled the covers over my head as the lights went out. Blanket lying at my feet, as was her usual spot.

I woke that morning to the voice of House.

"Call from Kit, should I tell her to hold?"

It took me a moment to come to my senses.

"Uh, no. Answer call. Hello?" I said, now speaking to Kit.

"Hey, got your text last night saying you'd be coming. So should we meet at your house?"

"Huh? My house, why?" I was still waking up, plus my head felt like someone had hammered it all night.

"Are you okay? Did I wake you up?"

"Umm, okay, sorta," I mumbled, "And yeah you did kinda wake me up."

"What do you mean 'sorta'? Is it your head again? Do you still wanna go shopping?"

"Yes, it's my head again," I confessed, she knew everything, "And yes, I still wanna shop. Meet me outside of the lab in like, thirty minutes, okay?"

She was quiet for a moment; I got up and grabbed some fresh clothes. Then heard her say thoughtfully, "Have you tried painkillers?"

I nodded, and then remembered she couldn't see me. "Yes, they never helped."

"Wow," another moments silence, then, "See ya in thirty minutes then." She hung up.

"House, please make me and Blanket some kind of breakfast."

After I took a quick shower, Blanket and I went downstairs to eat. I was watching the daily newscast when House informed me that my guests had arrived.

"Let them in and tell them to come on upstairs."

The weather came on; they said it would be a beautiful day tomorrow, a wonderful day for fireworks.

I heard the elevator open as the newswoman

said, "Guess who's turning fifteen this Monday? The son of the world known scientist Dr. Forjd. Yep, that's right folks Kieth Forjd, also known as the most intelligent kid on earth is turning fifteen!"

I turned the television off; I didn't like the idea that my birthday was being announced on the news so that the whole world would know it.

"Oh that reminds me," Kit was behind me now along with her siblings and grandparents, "I have to get you a birthday present."

"No you don't," I said standing, putting my dishes in the sink.

"You know I'm ignoring you right?"

"Yes," I said glumly as I turned towards the back door, where we would find the car.

"Come with me, the car's this way." They followed me through the hall towards what I called our 'second garage'.

"House, please get the car." We entered the garage, it looked like it could fit three cars, but there was none to be found.

On the ground were some yellow warning lines that formed a large square. A moment later there was a beeping noise and what seemed to be solid ground vanished and up came the City Car from the floor. The City Car had no wheels, just a bar in the middle of the bottom of the car.

As soon as the beeping stopped I said, "Everyone pile in, I don't care where you sit."

"Drivers seat!" called Troy and Tezibell at the same time. They both raced toward the front left door of the SUV. Tezibell got there first.

"Ha-ha!" she laughed, "Looks like you get shotgun."

Troy stuck his tongue out at her but did as she said, "I get drivers seat on the way back though."

Kit and I filed into the back seats and let her grandparents get the middle seats.

"Allrighty," I said. "Where do y'all wanna go first?"

"The mall of course!" said Tezibell. "Okay, House, please take us to the Decatur mall."

The garage door opened and the car moved outside and onto the road. No one was driving it. It was a wonderful technology that ran the car. It allowed the driver to be worry-free while going place to place. Everyone in the upper cities had a City Car.

The cars drove on invisible lines that directed the car onto the path needed. There were no more accidents because it was so advanced that all the cars could go on it at once and could still get to their desired destination in a reasonable amount of time. Basically everything was automated.

"Time until arrival, ten minutes," said House. I sat back in my seat and relaxed.

"Your forehead looks better," Kit noted.

I had almost forgotten the scratches on my head. I slid my hand along my forehead gently and could tell the scratches were healing fast.

"I guess the Band-Aids must have fallen off while I was asleep."

"You sure do heal fast, the scratches are almost gone," she noted, then continued in a quieter voice, "How's your head?"

"Better."

"You have another dream?" she pondered.

"Yeah, same thing as last time. It's so frustrating."

"I'm sure it will go away sometime," she said matter-of-factly. "I hope you're right."

The car started to slow. When it stopped we all got out onto the sidewalk of the mall parking lot. Once the last person was out and the area around the car was clear it disappeared into the ground. The upper city acted like one huge garage, holding all the city's cars inside of its body when they were not in use.

Our small party walked into the mall. Everything was in a buzz, there were hundreds of people scurrying about, walking store to store. Some had shopping bags of different sizes in their hands; others had a hovering shopping cart strolling along behind them, laden with merchandise.

There was a faint smell of food in the air, coming from the direction of the food court no doubt. The mall was shaped in a large oval, It had multiple stores on either side of its oversized hallways; vendors of small products formed a line in the middle of these hallways.

The vendors were trying to get people to buy their random products like a new moisturizing lotion for men that had the extra option of some new hair growth formula in it, a phony I bet.

We all walked in awe for a few moments looking at all the wonderful stores and deciding which to enter first.

Finally Tezibell squealed with delight, "Look Kit! They're having a sale on boots!" She and Kit started running for the store.

"Wait girls," their Grandma hollered after them, they stopped and looked back.

"I'm sure the men don't want to look at girly boots, so how bout I go with y'all and we'll buy you each a new pair of boots. And then the boys can go look at what they want and we can all meet up later at the food court for lunch, agreed?"

"Yes," they said, as they continued to the boot store, leaving the men behind.

"Well boys, anything y'all wanna look at?" asked Kits grandpa.

"Electronics store?" Troy asked me.

"Why not," I shrugged.

We went to the near by map of the mall. I only glanced at it once, but I had it memorized.

"This way," I said heading in the direction we had come from. Troy and his grandpa followed me into the midst of the shoppers and vendors. We didn't have to walk too far before arriving at the electronics store.

It was cram-packed full of people, mostly teens, but there was more people in that store than I wanted to count.

"Must be something new in the market," said

Troy's grandpa.

Only then did I notice that most of the people were gathered around a platform where some man was demonstrating something that I could not see. We gathered closer to the platform. I noticed that the man on the platform seemed to have some sort of watch on his wrist. He was showing this watch to the eager crowd.

"This is no ordinary watch folks," I heard him say, "This is your iPod, cell phone, House System, anything you can imagine! All in one tiny little wrist watch. Observe."

The crowd gasped as he touched something on the watch and suddenly we all were seeing the sky outside.

"Holographic tech," I whispered, impressed.

Holographic technology was still new to the world, and was very hard to assemble. It had the ability so that you could not only see and hear the item it projected, but you could also smell, feel, and even taste the object. It was pretty awesome tech. But usually came with a pretty hefty price tag, so that only the certain people in the government could use them.

"Have you ever seen a thing like that!" said Troy.

I actually have seen it before, my Dad helped design it, but he quit before it was finished to go work on one of his own projects.

The man continued to show his audience the watch's many little nick-knacks.

Afterwards, he announced that they were now on

sale. Once he said that it seemed as if each and every person watching rushed to the poor cashier.

"Wish I could afford me one of those," Troy said as we walked out of the store, it was time to meet the girls in the food court.

The girls were already there, sitting at a table, waiting.

"Oh good, there y'all are," said Tezibell as she spotted us. "Now we can eat!"

In a few moments we were all seated around our small table eating some McDonalds meal. I had gotten a grilled chicken wrap, my favorite. The others either got a burger or a Happy Meal.

They were always kidding me about not liking burgers, how by not liking burgers I just wasn't a Texan.

"Sure is busy today," Kit said, she sat across from me, I was between the other boys.

"It's Fourth of July weekend, what did you expect, an empty mall?" I said this through a mouthful of chicken and tortilla.

"Well, I'm at least glad we got to get those boots that were on sale, now I have some nice new boots for my next competition."

After eating we traveled together and explored the many stores of the mall. Once we came upon the glow-in-the-dark mini golf, we couldn't resist and had to play. I tried very hard not to win. I had played the course before, so I knew how to get hole in ones on each hole.

Kit knew that and kept kidding me when I

purposely took four shots to get it in the hole.

When we came upon one of the hardest holes Kit said, "Come on, get a hole in one this time, just for this hole?"

I sighed, "Fine." I reluctantly walked up to the starting point and set the neon green golf ball I was using onto the floor. I didn't have to look at the course to hit the ball, but I did it anyway so as not to rouse suspicion.

The hole was at the other end of a series of 'L' shaped turns, that was hard in its self, but the toughest part was that the hole was under a swinging log shaped thing, so that if you didn't time your swing right the ball would be hit and sent in another direction.

I positioned the ball in the right place with my foot. Everyone was watching me. I waited until just the right moment then 'click' I swung the club and it hit the ball and sent it on its course towards the hole.

I watched as the ball ricochet off the sidings of the 'L' shaped turns then everyone around me gasped as the ball rolled into the hole.

"Told ya he could do it," Kit whispered to Troy.

I allowed myself a small smile as the others took their turns attempting what I did. They kept asking how I had done it.

I simply replied, "Positioning and timing is key."

Turns out my efforts to try and lose worked, Kits grandpa won. Troy and Tezibell tied for second leaving Kit with third and me with fourth, right where I wanted to be. Kit's grandma didn't play; she preferred to watch instead.

It was at least three o'clock by the time we finished our putt-putt game. We decided to walk around a little longer, but after an hour or so more, we tuckered out and decided that it was time to leave.

When we arrived back at the house we all had a slightly lighter wallet. Everyone had gotten something except me. All I had bought was my lunch and putt-putt admission.

Being a good host, I asked if they would like to stay for dinner. They declined, saying that Kit's mom had something planned.

I followed them down to the Lower Level to where they would take their manual car back home. Dad, who was down in the lab, surprisingly asked us how our day of shopping had been.

We all replied that it had been good.

Kit then asked him, "You are going to come over tomorrow to celebrate Kieth's Birthday, right?"

Dad smiled, "Of course, wouldn't miss it for the world."

"Good," she smiled back, "See y'all tomorrow." she hopped into the car where everyone else was waiting for her.

We waved as they left the driveway. Once they left Dad jokingly said, "Cute girl, that Kit. Sure has a bubbly personality."

I turned back towards the Lab then said, "She's just a good friend, that's all." "But you still don't want to leave her, am I right?" he called to me.

I stopped and turning my head back towards him I said, "No, I don't want to leave her. She's my best friend." I continued walking and whispered under my breath, "My only friend."

Dad had me depressed now. The whole rest of the night I kept thinking about the trip and how much I wished I could just stay where I felt most at home.

Chapter 6
The Party

Later the next day, I biked over to Kits, Blanket tagging along as usual. That morning I had decided to dress for the occasion, a red, white, and blue T-shirt that had the American flag on it. I even decided to put a blue bandana around Blankets neck.

Before leaving the house I had asked Dad if he wanted to go early with me, but he declined saying he'd be over later.

Everything had changed from the other night. When I arrived at the porch of the house it was decorated with every patriotic thing you could imagine, from flags to streamers.

I found that the same thing had happened as I entered the house. Everywhere I looked was red, white and blue. The Friesians always went over the top at their get-togethers.

"Happy Fourth!" I said as I spotted Kit and Troy, both on stools, putting up a banner over the table. "Looks like y'all have been busy."

"Yes, we have," Kit said.

Troy added, "Since after dinner last night... A little higher, Sis," he instructed to Kit.

"Wow, is there anything I can do to help?"

"Yeah, hand me that tape, there on the table, please."

I grabbed it and tore a piece off for Kit to use. She taped it, and then hopped off her stool.

"There, that looks good."

Now that they had it up I could see what the banner said, it read 'Happy Fourth of July!' and under that it read 'Happy Fifteenth B-day Kieth!'.

"Who all did you invite again?" I said nervously, by the way all the decorations looked, it seemed she could have invited a lot.

"Just the usual group," she said casually.

The 'usual group' was all her, and her family's friends from church. I'd seen them all before but didn't know them personally. Though I should, they were all over often enough.

"When did you tell them all to arrive?"

"They will all be here soon, actually," she said looking at the clock.

I followed them outside to where everyone else was. They were putting up tiny U.S flags all over the lawn.

"Where do you get all these decorations?" I asked as we started helping put the rest of the flags in the dirt.

Kit shrugged, "Craft stores, online, I don't know, anywhere we can find them I guess."

Once finished, we sat around in lawn chairs waiting for the guests to arrive. A few minutes later, two cars came down the driveway.

I recognized the cars, the first was that of the Parr's, and the second belonged to the Warner's.

They both parked in the loop of the driveway. Two kids piled out of the Parr's car. The first was a girl with blonde hair; her name was Nyleta. She ran over to Tezibell and gave her a big hug. She always had a smile on her face.

The second was a boy with cropped brown hair. His name was Tawy. He walked over to where Troy was; he had something in his hands.

Out of the Warner's car came another two kids, a boy, and a girl. The boys name was Scrip.

He went over to join Troy and Tawy.

The girl, Ella, walked over to Tezibell and Nyleta and they went off to go and talk.

The kid's parents went over to chat with Kit's parents.

We were about to join them when another car came down the drive.

"Oh my gosh! It's Annie!" Kit said running over to the car, in which Annie had just come out of.

Annie was one of Kit's best friends, like they knew each other since they were two years old kind of best friend.

They gave each other a hug.

"I missed you!" Kit said, releasing her.

Annie chuckled, "I wasn't gone that long."

"I know that."

"Hey, Kieth!" Annie said as she saw me, "I haven't seen you in a long while."

"Yeah, long time no see; how have you been?" I told her.

"I've been well, thank you." She paused a moment and then said, "Hey! Look what I brought!" She reached into the front seat of her car and brought out a large container full of pretzels.

"Oh my gosh! Are those what I think they are?" Kit exclaimed, reaching for the container.

"They might be. But you gotta catch me to find out." and with that Annie took off at a run with the container of pretzels. Kit ran after her. I followed, not exactly sure why there was such a big fuss over a container of pretzels.

I soon found out though that they were not indeed pretzels but *spicy* pretzels. I could only describe them in one word.

Amazing.

They tasted exactly like chips with salsa on them and very soon we all had to go get a cup of water cause we had eaten too many of them and our tongues were now burning off.

After we got a refreshments Kit said, "Who wants to go bareback riding to the tank and swim a little while before we eat?"

Annie and I both thought it was a great idea for it was very hot outside.

Before we headed off, we made sure it was all right with Kit's parents. They said it was okay but to be cautious of snakes and other various critters.

So we all got on a horse. I was on Cowboy again and Kit and Annie were riding double on Image.

We didn't take any reins to go to the tank so Kit and Image lead and somehow Cowboy followed. I was just along for the ride, Blanket trudging along behind us.

I kept twisting Cowboys black mane around in my fingers until we arrived at the tank.

The tank was only deep enough to cover the horses backs, but it was still fun to swim in.

Without hesitating, the horses trotted into the refreshing green water. They didn't stop until the water was over their backs and into the pants of their riders.

Lucky for me, I had kicked off my boots before Cowboy ran into the tank.

For the first few minutes in the tank, we amused ourselves by splashing each other with water. Then Kit started the fun.

She, Annie, and Image went into the deeper water while I stayed in the shallows with Blanket and watched as Kit and Annie both attempted to stand on Images back. They fell backwards, halfway through attempting to stand.

They came up laughing, wet hair in their faces; I joined in on their laughter. Then I urged Cowboy out to the deep and attempted to stand. I was also unsuccessful.

We each tried multiple times but every time one of us almost got it, we were laughing so hard that we just fell.

Eventually we headed back to the house, all sopping wet, to eat some food with the others.

While we had been at the tank Dad had arrived at the party and I saw him standing with the other adults. I didn't think that my scientist of a father looked comfortable around these 'laid back' simple country folk.

We had some fajitas that Mr. Friesian cooked up

on an old fashioned grill. They were delicious. (We also had an uncountable number of spicy pretzels.)

After eating we decided to head back to the tank, but Kit's parents caught me before we could leave and decided to sing happy birthday.

Mrs. Friesian brought out a chocolate cake she must have made; it had fifteen candles on it that she lit.

Everyone was around me, and the cake, now and they began to sing happy birthday.

Once the last words died, I made a wish and blew out the candles. Then they decided to give me my presents.

I didn't get much, mostly gift cards to places, but I appreciated the thoughts and thanked everyone for the gifts.

After that was over Kit, Annie, and I went to go hop on the horses again. Troy, Tezibell, and their friends decided to join us.

They had gotten three more horses out of the barn. That way no one had to walk to the pond. We did have to put three people on the strongest horse though.

Tawy sat behind me all the way to the tank. When we arrived everyone took off their boots or tennis shoes and ran into the water.

Troy had the great idea of playing water freeze tag. Everyone agreed immediately.

They chose the person to be 'it' by saying it'd be the birthday boy. So I started to count to ten under water, holding up my hands so that everyone else could see where I was in counting.

When I came up out of the water I quickly tagged Tezibell as she swam past my feet. "Gotcha!" I said as she resurfaced.

"Whoa! How'd you see me under the water?" she asked as she put her hands in the air, indicating she was frozen.

I just shrugged and continued to tag people.

Surprisingly, I won the round and then it was Troy's turn to be it.

When Troy was done counting he immediately went after Kit, who was only a few feet from him.

He tagged her then went on to the next closest. I swam over to Kit and dove in the water so I could swim underneath her to unfreeze her. Upon resurfacing a hand touched my head; it was Troy.

"Tag!" he then went racing after Kit again as I put my arms in the air.

We kept playing freeze tag until the sun started setting. That's when the parents joined us. They brought along with them a load-full of fireworks. Once it was too dark to see we all got out of the water and went to go lay down on towels so that we could watch the dads light the fireworks.

But before they lit them Kit's Grandpa wanted to say a thing or two about what the Fourth of July meant to him.

"The Fourth of July," he began, "As you already know, is an American holiday. But we Texans still celebrate it with our sister country America because the Fourth is more than just food and fireworks. On this day, over thousand of years ago, our great fore fathers signed the Declaration of Independence and in doing that they made America a free country. America took us in when we could not protect ourselves from others. And as you know, Texas finally became strong enough about a hundred years ago to protect its own boundaries and decided to become its own country again. Well that's my brief history lesson of the day, now how bout we all sing Americas national anthem."

With that, we all stood from where we had been sitting and placed our hands over our hearts and sung the national anthem. We all sung it as if it were our own national anthem.

Once finished, the men headed to the other side of the tank so they could start the fireworks.

I watched as they lit the first one. They all ran away from it as it shot up into the air with a whooshing sound and exploded into a brilliant sparkle of lights. There were multiple 'oohs' and 'aahs' as the fireworks display continued.

Once all the fireworks had been shot off, Kit's dad gave us each a Roman Candle. We shot them across the tank. It was so much fun to watch and do.

The last thing we did were sparklers. They were fun because we dared each other to walk back (the horses roamed free so therefore had left us ages ago) to the house by only the light of our long lasting sparklers.

We all did it of course, screaming and giggling the whole way back as we attempted to sing Yankee

Doodle and other fun patriotic songs.

After finally arriving back at the house, sparklers growing dim, we were all tuckered out, so we sat on the grass waiting for the parents to come back so we could go home.

I sat and chatted with Kit and Annie, we talked about the game of freeze tag.

Kit was saying, "And remember when I was it and just literally jumped into you Annie!"

"Oh yeah," I said with a laugh, "I saw that, it was hilarious."

We continued to laugh at all the fun things that happened that day, even if it wasn't that funny.

Finally the parents arrived. Dad was with them and the moment he got out of the car they had ridden in, I could tell just by looking at his face that he was ready to leave.

So I got up and went to go put my bike into the back of the truck. Kit and Annie followed me.

"What are you doing?" Kit asked.

"My dad's ready to leave, so I'm gonna put my bike into the bed of the truck."

Dad was already in the truck by the time I'd placed the bike in the bed. I sighed, time to say goodbyes.

I walked over to where everyone else had gathered, some also saying goodbye.

"You disappear at the most unusual times dog," I said as I noticed Blanket trailing behind me. She had left before the fireworks and now she was back again.

First I went to Mr. and Mrs. Friesian to thank them for the party and for the food; they said it was no big deal. Then I went around to thank everyone else for the gifts and to say goodbye.

Lastly I said goodnight to Kit.

I walked up to her and gave her a hug, "Thank you," I whispered in her ear.

"For what?" she asked as I released her, clearly startled.

"For one of the best birthday parties I've had in a long while."

"Oh that," she joked, "It was nothing."

"Well, it wasn't nothing to me."

I heard a horn honk and realized Dad was getting impatient.

"Gotta go, I'll talk to you later, oh and nice to see you again Annie," I quickly said as I ran off to the truck.

I hopped into the passengers seat; Dad took off down the driveway.

"I approve of her, you know if you ever want to take it to the next level," Dad joked as we got onto the road.

Annoyed I answered, "She still just a friend Dad." He just chuckled.

When we got home, I realized Blanket wasn't there. I saw her get into the bed, but she was nowhere to be seen. So I called her name, no one came.

"Dad, I can't find Blanket." I said still calling her name.

"I'm sure she's still at the Friesians house, she'll be fine," he reassured me, although there was slight a hint of worry on his face.

Chapter 7
Unexpected Events

I woke that morning, without realizing exactly what day it was. It took a phone call from Kit to remind me it was my birthday.

After I spoke with her, I lay on my bed, a hand behind my head. I was thinking back to when I first started to remember everything. I did this every year on my birthday. It was kind of like watching old home videos, but I didn't have to share them with anyone.

My birthdays had always been kind of sad to me because they reminded me of Mom. I didn't know much about her though, she died giving birth to me. Dad practically was my mother and father.

As I got to the beginning of my mental 'home videos' I struggled to remember Mom's face. But as always when I tried, I never could come up with any picture other than the pictures Dad had given me.

I took one of those pictures out now, and just stared at it. All I knew about her was her name, Atia, and what she looked like in this picture. She had gold brown hair and hazel eyes. I thought she was beautiful.

Dad never talked about her, never told me what she was like, or who she was, or anything. All I had were the pictures.

After a few minutes of staring at the photos, I realized tears were slowly rolling down my cheeks.

I put the pictures down and wiped the tears away, then got up to get dressed.

I was still kinda somber as I walked downstairs to go and eat breakfast.

It got even worse as I found Dad rushing around the place.

"What are you doing?" I asked, as he walked off to the garage with a box of paperwork.

"Gather the rest of your things, we're leaving now."

"Wait, what do you mean we're leaving now? Leaving where?" I followed him into the garage, the City Car was sitting there waiting, doors open, our things inside of it.

After putting the box into the car, Dad turned and looked me in the eyes, "We are leaving now to go to the airport, then from there, Alaska."

"Wait," I said. I was hearing him, but not believing him. "Today? But we are supposed to leave on the 16th! Why do we possibly have to leave now?"

He walked past me back towards the kitchen, "There's been a change of plans."

"Obviously!" I shouted after him.

Why? Why did the plans change? Why now?

I walked back to the kitchen. Dad was gathering more paperwork.

A sudden thought occurred to me, "What about Blanket? I need to go look for her."

"I'm sure if she's at your friend's house she will be taken care of." There was no hint of worry on his face anymore.

"So now I can't even say goodbye?!" I yelled.

"No." he said simply, "We have to leave now in order to catch the plane. Now run upstairs and gather your things."

When I made no movement to go upstairs he yelled, "Hustle now!"

Defeated and even more somber than when I had come down, I ran upstairs to gather my things.

I didn't need much; we were getting more clothes in Alaska. All I grabbed was my personal things, like my dream journal, and pictures.

"Hurry up Kieth!" Dad yelled up the stairs.

What had triggered this change in him? Just last night he was joking about Kit and me and now he was all in a 'hustle bustle' to get to the airport!

Speaking of Kit, what would I tell her? I decided to text her when I got into the car.

'I won't be able to come over today...' I wrote as we left the garage and cruised onto the road. It was only nine o'clock. But there was no one out on the streets.

'Y not?' she asked.
'leaving'
'where to?'
'airport'
'WHAT!!!!WHY??'
'Change of plans'
'why!!' she asked again.
'I've got no clue... on a completely unrelated

note, have you seen my dog??'

'No... WHY!!!'

'He didn't tell me why... Tell me if you see her plz!'

'your trying to change the subject KF!'

'No I'm not' Yes, I was but I didn't want to talk about Alaska, let alone go there.

'yes, you are. And of course I'll take care of her if she appears' She always knew what I was thinking.

'thnks. :) '

That was the end of our conversation for a while. I got bored quickly, we didn't have far to go, only thirty minutes, but it seemed like forever to me.

I felt like this was going to be the last time I would see my hometown...

Everything might be completely different when I came back.... *If* I came back.

Finally, we arrived at the airport. We paid a guy to get the luggage. The only thing we had to do was get through security and onto the plane in time. Which with Dad being who he was, it wasn't that hard.

We then sat down and waited to board the plane. I took to watching the people that walked by while Dad had his nose in some book. After a while, I decided to go get something to eat, having skipped breakfast in the rush that morning.

I stood in one of the horribly long lines with many other hungry people when it happened. Some girl bumped into me, knocking me over.

While on my bum, rubbing my head, something fell into my lap. It was a decorative box with a bow on it. I got up quickly, thinking it was the girl's but when I looked around, I didn't see her.

I held onto the box and after getting my meal I walked around the terminal looking for her. I had gotten a good enough glimpse of the girl to know what she looked like, and the funny thing was, she looked vaguely familiar. I looked all over the place but didn't see her.

Eventually Dad texted me saying that it was time to go. Sighing, I pocketed the package and turned towards the terminal.

I was the last one on the plane. I quickly found my seat next to Dad and then took out the package. I looked to see if there was any name on it. I was surprised to find my own name as the recipient.

"What's that you got there?" Dad asked, looking up from his book.

"I don't know yet."

"Well tell me when you do," and with that he was back in his book. But then he said, "Happy Birthday by the way."

I decided to open it, I gasped as I saw that it was a high tech watch.

"Who..," I started, then realized Dad wasn't listening. There was a note, it read.

'Happy Birthday Chosen One!'

Chosen one? Okay, maybe not for me. I read on.

'Enjoy the watch. Cost me a hand and foot to get this. Also, Alaska may not be as bad as you might think.

Be seeing you soon,
~F
P.S. I'll be watching you, little brother.'

Okay, maybe a little creepy. The plane readied to taxi out onto the runway.

My stomach did a full back flip as I realized too late what was happening. We were about to fly.

I quickly texted Kit, 'Goodbye...'

'Goodbye.' she wrote back, 'We'll miss you...'

I turned off my phone and prepared for the flight by trying to sleep. I'll miss you too, I thought, as the plane slowly rose into the air.

I was on my way to Alaska.

Chapter 8
Secrets in Anchorage

I dared not look out the window for the six hours I was confined to the airplane. Failing to fall asleep, unlike Dad who had abandoned his book, I fiddled around with my new watch. It was pretty awesome. I could take pictures and videos and later, when we landed, I could use it as a phone.

Around lunchtime the flight attendants came around asking if anyone would like a sandwich. I got two, one for me and one for Dad, who I woke up.

"Here's lunch," I said giving him the sandwich.

"Thank you," we both took out our trays and gobbled down the sandwiches.

A few hours later the pilot told everyone to put on their seat belts, we had arrived in Anchorage.

I gladly put it on, closed my eyes, and held on for dear life until we were safely on the ground.

The moment the wheels of the plane touched the runway my head began to ache. I knew then that this would not be a good trip.

"Time to get out Kieth," Dad said when everyone was up getting their things. I still had my eyes shut.

I unbuckled, then stood but fell back into the seat instantly, I held my swaying head.

"Are you okay?" Dad asked me.

"Yeah," I lied, "Just dizzy from flying is all."

I stood again, this time staying on my feet. I was surprised that I made it out of the plane, through the small airport, and into the car that was waiting for us outside, without falling over.

Everything seemed to sway as we drove away from the airport, like I was riding a boat on rocky waves. It made me sick to my stomach. I tried to lean my head back and closing my eyes, but it only made it worse.

Every time I closed my eyes, I saw things, I wouldn't know how to explain it, but I saw things that weren't there; shouldn't be there...

Dad, who was again sitting next to me, asked, "Are you sure your all right? You look pale."

I slowly shook my head. I couldn't contain my pain any longer.

"No, I'm terribly dizzy and my head hurts like crazy." I felt a hand on my back.

"Hold on, we're almost to the house where we're staying."

Once we arrived Dad guided me out of the car and into the house. I didn't take in much of what happened or what anything looked like, for every time I blinked images flashed through my head.

I heard something about 'lying down' and 'flying doesn't agree with him' before falling into an uneasy sleep.

I woke up, what seemed like hours later, on a bed inside of a room that smelled and looked like fresh wood. Looking out of the tiny window told me that it must be evening.

I sat up, my head still felt as if it was at war with

itself, but I thankfully no longer saw the images of things I couldn't understand. The images though, still filled my head. I checked my watch; it was 6:41pm on July the 7th. The seventh! I stood, but regretted it quickly as I nearly passed out from the sudden change in elevation. I lay back down, the vertigo starting to fade away. I'd been out for at least two days! Maybe I was sick? The only thing that was wrong was my head hurt, but still, I shouldn't be out for two days!

After a moment the vertigo completely went away, but I still lay there until finally my stomach, and curiosity, lead me outside of the room and into a hallway lined with pictures of people I didn't know.

I took a left, I heard familiar voices talking, speaking to one another. I slowly walked out into a room that must have been a living room slash kitchen. It had a few couches scattered around the room, along with a bar that had a sink and all the other good kitchen amenities.

Dad and another man were sitting around a large dining table. I recognized the other man as Mr. Newark. That's weird; I didn't know he would be here.

I stood in the door of the hallway for a few moments, resting my head on the doorframe, and spied on them. They seemed to be in an important conversation that had to do something with a book they had. I heard only some of their conversation.

"You think we'll find her here?" Mr. Newark was

saying.

"Yes, this is one of the last places she was seen."

"And you think he'll be able to help us find her?"

"As I've already told you, he doesn't yet have a mark, but he shows potential."

Just then Dad saw me standing there and quickly hid the book from view.

"Good evening Kieth, have a nice nap?" he said. He clearly knew I had been standing there for a while but he didn't bring it up.

I walked up to the table like nothing happened, and said, "Yes." My voice sounded froggy, I cleared my throat then addressed Mr. Newark, "I didn't know you'd be here."

Mr. Newark stood and shook my hand, "I had the extra time so I decided to come and help your father with the expedition." He sat back down and chuckled.

"What's so funny?" I asked, taking the seat opposite Dad.

"Oh nothing, it's just how is it you, being the..." he paused, searching for the right word, "*Thing* that you are, can't take a simple plane ride?"

"Thing?" I asked, offended. When had I become a 'thing'?

Dad glared at Mr. Newark, "How bout some dinner, Nexryt?"

"Thing?" I asked again, this time a little louder. Dinner was far from my mind; I wasn't going to let this go so easily.

Mr. Newark was clearly regretting what he had

said, "Yes! Let's have some dinner," with that he got up and headed off to the kitchen.

"What does he mean by 'thing' Dad?"

"He doesn't mean *anything*," he answered before getting up and heading off to the kitchen too, leaving me alone at the table.

I'll never get answers out of anyone today! I arose from the chair and walked outdoors, ignoring the cold air that chilled my bare arms. I started walking away from the house.

But I stopped; tears started forming in my eyes as I realized I had nowhere to go to. No escaping to Kit's house to ride horses, no Blanket to cuddle up with, I had nobody to go to. Sure, I could text Kit, but I didn't want to trouble her with my loneliness, and that wasn't the same as actually seeing her.

So I just stood there, letting the loneliness engulf my mind. Eventually, I calmed myself by using a breathing technique I had learned in my years of taking karate. But I still sat there on the ground not caring enough to go inside to eat.

As I sat there I thought of what Dad and Mr. Newark had been saying. Who had they been talking about? Obviously a guy and a girl. Apparently the girl disappeared and they are looking for her, but who was this guy who is supposed to help find her. As far as I knew there was only the three of us here so far.

A door opening and closing interrupted my thoughts. Footsteps came towards me, I didn't bother looking around to see who it was, I already knew it was Dad.

He put a hand on my shoulder, "Come inside, son, you have to eat."

I shrugged off his hand, "Not until you tell me what Mr. Newark meant by calling me a 'thing'."

I heard him sigh, "He didn't mean any harm; he was just referring to how smart you are."

I didn't believe him; the way Mr. Newark had said it made me think it was something else. But I didn't bring it up. It was beginning to darken outside; I hadn't realized I'd been out for that long.

"Come now, we've made some chicken soup," he held out his hand to me, I grasped it and he pulled me up. I held my head as the world started to tilt. Dad grabbed me before I could fall over.

"Can you walk?"

"I probably could, but I might fall on my face a few times." He held onto me and guided me towards the house to make sure I didn't fall over.

"Do you know what's wrong with me?" I asked, thinking he just might know.

"We had the local doctor come by and take a look at you when you didn't wake up. I told him how you said you felt, and he said that you probably had a busted ear drum and that's why you're so dizzy."

We entered the house and it was defiantly warmer than it was outside. Immediately we were greeted with the smell of chicken soup.

"But that doesn't explain why I was out for two days," I said as he sat me down in a chair.

He got me a bowl of soup; it looked delicious. Steam rose from the bowl so I waited a moment for it to cool down.

"You apparently had an ear infection, and your ear drum must have burst as we landed. The thing that gets me though is that he said your head should have been hurting because of the infection even before it burst. Is this true?"

It didn't sound like this is what was wrong with me, but then again, it did. I didn't want to confess that my head had been hurting, but he had me in a pickle.

"Yes, it's true." I slurped down a spoonful of soup, I again remembered how hungry I was, and began to slurp the soup down even faster.

"Why didn't you tell me?"

"I didn't want to worry you."

He was quiet for a moment, while I continued to eat.

"Next time, tell me when you're not feeling well so we can avoid what has happened, agreed?"

"Agreed," I got a second helping of soup.

"So what have you been up to since I fell asleep?" I asked after I finished.

"We have been searching around the area, but now I'm not too sure if Anchorage is where we need to be," he trailed off, then took my bowl and brought it to the kitchen sink.

"Not more planes?" I complained. I'd had enough of them.

He chuckled, "No, we won't go anywhere till

your ear heals up, then if we do decide to leave we'll find other means of transportation."

"That's good" We were both silent for a few minutes, I started nodding off.

"Let's get you to bed." Dad said. He helped me to my room and into bed. I fell asleep as soon as my head hit the pillow.

That night I dreamed about the girl who had bumped into me. I dreamed we were in a forest walking along an unknown trail; the girl seemed to know where she was going. I followed her. Looking behind me, another girl was tagging along. The girl in front turned around and said something to us. I woke up as I saw her face.

"Fauna," I whispered, I knew who she was now. It was the girl from the nightmare that had started this series of unfortunate events. But how could she even be real? Was it all a coincidence? Did the girl who gave me the watch just happen to look like the girl from my dreams? And if it was real, what did it all mean?

I didn't dare think about it any longer. My head throbbed, as I got dressed. It was tolerable though.

Dad and Mr. Newark were already in the kitchen eating breakfast. I grabbed myself some then sat down and ate it all without saying a word to them. I was still kinda angry with Mr. Newark.

After finishing I asked, "Can I go walk around the place?"

"If you think you can make it back home without crawling then yes." That was all I needed.

I rushed out the door, but not before grabbing a sweater and a hat from my room.

I explored a little bit outside the house, there wasn't much. But I did happen upon a bike, which looked rideable. There was a town nearby the house so I took the bike for a spin.

A sign outside the town read 'Lower Anchorage'. There must be an Upper Anchorage nearby.

Before entering the town I made sure my hat was covering all my hair. I didn't want to be recognized, and recognized I would be if people got a glimpse of my red hair. I rode on down through the town, people were out and about, there was a bunch of manual vehicles about the place trying to get to their destination.

I stayed on the sidewalk, trying to avoid the cars. I saw many stores along the streets. From food outlets to antique stores, there was everything. I rode around the whole town until I was sure I'd seen everything.

In the town was, a small school, a hospital, and church. It was all very different from the way that I was used to living. Everything just seemed smaller. I would have stayed to eat lunch, but I had no money with me so I went back to the house.

No one was home when I arrived back, there was a note on the table.

-Gone to town to recruit helpers for our expedition, lunch is in fridge. See you later, Dad-

As he said, there was leftover chicken soup in the fridge. I heated this up, then went to my room to eat it.

After eating I decided to see what Kit was doing.

'hey' I wrote, using my new watch as my phone.

She quickly replied, 'Hey! I've called you just about a gazillion times! Where have you been?'

'I was sick... Eardrum burst or something. Sorry I didn't text you sooner.' I felt like I should say something more, but decided against it.

'I was worried... Are you better now?'

'Ya I'm better now', it didn't feel right talking to her when we were so far away from each other.

'Did you find her?' I asked, referring to Blanket. I was starting to get terribly homesick.

'Sorry, no. We haven't seen any sign of her.'

I sighed, why did this have to happen to me? Losing all those I cared about.

Kit and I exchanged a few more texts, and then she had to go. I lay on the bed for a little while, thinking about home, until I decided that thinking about things I couldn't change would only make me glum.

So I got up and walked around the house. It was a pretty big house, I explored every inch of it.

Finally at the end of my exploring, I reached the room that had been transformed into a lab area. I was about to just leave the room alone, but something drew me into it. The room had many tables filled with countless books and notebook papers.

I walked up to one of these tables and picked up one of its books. This, however, wasn't a book but a notebook, and it looked well used.

As I looked it over more closely I realized that this was the book that Dad and Mr. Newark had been fussing over. I shuffled through the pages; there was writing all over it.

Suddenly I heard the door open. I quickly put the book back down and turned around, Dad was coming through the door. Surprise flashed upon his face as he saw me.

"What are you doing in here?" he asked with a hint of anger.

"I was exploring the house."

"Exploring or snooping?"

"I didn't touch anything. I was just having a look around the place."

He seemed to relax a little, but he was still tense. "I don't want to find you in here anymore, understood?"

"Yes." I walked out of the room under his watchful eye. I wanted to ask him why I couldn't go in there, but I knew that would just make him even angrier, so I decided to just let that go.

Dinner was quiet that night; no one seemed to want to speak to each other, unless it was to pass the salt and pepper. Finally, after watching the nightly news in my room, I went to sleep.

Chapter 9
You!

Things soon formed into a daily routine for me. Get up, take the bike to town, eat lunch at random food places, ride around till dinner, and go to bed.

I became bored very quickly.

Dad and Mr. Newark were always locked inside the lab, the only time I saw them was at breakfast and dinner.

The only thing that kept me from hitch hiking all the way back to Texas was my dreams. I kept dreaming about the girl, Fauna. The dream took place in a schoolyard that I later recognized as the schoolyard that was in town.

After realizing this, I visited the schoolyard every day after lunch, and just sat there till it was time to leave. I didn't know what lead me to do this. Maybe some part of my body believed that she would miraculously appear, just like in my dream.

I didn't expect anyone to appear, but I sat and waited anyway. I had nothing else to do.

As the days passed by, the sun started to set earlier and earlier. Soon enough it was September.

One chilly day I had sat down on an old swing set, I was eating my lunch as I usually did.

Everything seemed as if it would be the same as the days before. The children of Old Anchorage School would come out and play in a few minutes, as they were released from the pressures of learning.

Today they were a little late. I watched them from behind the swings, where I was hiding, as they filed out of the building. They all ran past their teachers who were leading them outside.

I casually got up from where I was hiding as the kids ran past me and got back onto the swing. Old Anchorage School taught kids from kindergarten up so I could easily pass as one of the tenth graders, but I still wore my hat so I didn't stand out to the teachers.

I swung back and forth on my swing, watching all of the kids run around the field with their friends. Some teenagers were out playing a game of kick ball. The smaller children were in a makeshift sandbox building sandcastles (really more like sand-mountains with holes in the middle).

The sound of squealing laughter reached my ears, I looked over to where some kids were playing freeze tag. Seeing the kids play reminded me of when I played the very same game in the pond with Kit on the Fourth of July.

I realized how long ago that had been, that was the last time I had seen her.

Stop thinking about it! You'll just ruin your day!

I swung higher and higher, trying to forget, but at the same time trying to pretend I was back in Texas.

If I were there now, we'd be trying to get in one more swim before the cool air came to Texas. It felt like an icicle here, and I knew as the days passed, it would just keep getting colder.

If I were there now, I would be at her house helping to decorate for fall, not here in this schoolyard on a swing, chasing a dream.

That's it! I'm going back to the house. I let go my grip of the swing, when I was at its highest, and glided off. "Ooof..." I landed right in the middle of a group of girls, and on top of one of them. I jumped up fast, trying not to crush the girl I had actually landed on.

"Oh my gosh!" I probably just broke her arm or something!

She wore thick winter pants and a hoodie that covered her face. She still lay on the ground, I reached out my hand to hers, helping her onto her feet.

"I'm so sor-" I let go of her hand; she fell back to the ground with a thump. Her hoodie fell off, revealing her face. All of a sudden

I was living my dream.

"You!"

Chapter 10
Questions Left Unanswered

There she was, just like my dream, smiling at me as if saying 'who else'.

In the blink of an eye she was up and swiftly running away from the schoolyard.

"Hey! Come back here!" I yelled, running after her.

She quickly ran around the school and towards the outskirts of the city. I followed at a full run, ditching my bike, for I was afraid I'd lose sight of her if I went to get it.

I seemed to be gaining on her but I could not stop her yet, I was too far away to touch her. I chased her all the way outside of the cities limits before I was able to dive and tackle her legs. I hung on tightly to her, as we slid a few feet in the mud. My whole front became muddy.

When we stopped, I quickly pinned her down to the ground before she could get up and run away again. Neither of us said a thing, we were panting too hard to get any words out. I just stared at her until my breathing finally slowed down enough for me to choke something out, "What-are you-doing here?"

She heaved a sigh; I could see the faint fog coming from her mouth. Her long brown hair was plastered to parts of her face, as she blew some out of her mouth. She gave a little laugh, resting her head on the ground.

"You're faster than you look!"

I ignored her, "How did you find me?"

She did not answer my question. I gave her a little shake.

"How do you know who I am?" I asked this with a little bit of desperation in my voice. I was utterly confused. She was real.

She looked at me with familiar green eyes and said, "I think the more important question here is how do you know who I am?"

I let her go, I was defeated. I expected her to run off but she just sat there watching me. I didn't want to answer; she would think me crazy if I did.

"Well, don't leave me hanging. I asked you a question and I expect you to answer it. See I think I deserve an answer after you've run me over three times."

I gave her a funny look. "Three times? If I remember correctly you ran me over the first time."

She smiled; she didn't seem to want to run away anymore, "Okay, I guess that was me the first time."

She pointed to my watch. "I see you like your present."

"Yes, it's very useful, um, thank you for getting it for me." It felt very odd talking to her; I hardly knew who she was.

"You still didn't answer my question," she said after a moment's silence.

"Well, you still haven't answered mine," I countered. It almost felt like I was talking to an old friend, someone I knew, but haven't seen in a long time.

Neither of us spoke, I didn't want to say anything else. It was getting late and I needed to head back to the house. Now I just needed to figure out how to ditch this girl.

Fauna stood, interrupting my thoughts. Good, maybe I don't have to ditch her after all. She reached her hand out towards me. "Let's start over," she said. I took her hand; she helped me up. "My name is Fauna, though, I think you already know that."

We kinda shook hands. "Kieth Forjd, and I think you knew that too."

"Yes, I did." She smiled, tucking her hair behind an ear.

"Well, uh, I gotta go and get my bike." Before I met her I had so many questions, but now that I knew she was real, I didn't know what to say.

"You can come with me, I guess."

"Ok," she said.

It didn't take too long to get back to the schoolyard, where I had left my bike. All the kids where gone, recess being over.

We walked across the school field, past the swings, and over to the fence line, where my bike was parked.

I wiped some mud off my jacket, how was I going to explain this to Dad?

I mounted the bike,

"Well, I guess this is goodbye?"

She didn't say anything for a moment. She

seemed to be thinking hard about something. I began to wonder if she would say anything at all.

Finally she said, "I'll meet you in town tomorrow, for lunch, and then I'll tell you what you want to know."

Then she ran off.

"Bye," I whispered, then peddled off in the direction of the house.

Chapter 11
Destination Barrow

"What happened to your clothes?" Darn, he had caught me as I tried to sneak into the house.

He was staring at me from the kitchen, while I thought I could sneak up to my room without him noticing.

"I fell off my bike, and into the mud." I lied, hoping he would take the bait.

He looked me over, probably thinking I had purposely rolled in mud. But he took the bait.

"Fine, go wash up, dinner's almost ready."

"What are we having?" "Chinese."

Dad always made good Chinese food so I hurried to my room to wash my face and change into some clean clothes. I came back out a moment later to the smell of chow-mien.

As I came through the hallway I noticed there were more voices then just Dad and Mr. Newark.

Who could be here?

I walked into the kitchen and quickly found out who the voices belonged to. There, taking off their winter coats, was a young man and young woman no older than twenty. Dinner was already on the table, Dad showed them to their seats.

As I neared the table, they both stood back up very quickly, like something had shocked their chairs. They both had city kid looks to them. The woman had short bubble gum pink hair; where-as the man had hair that was vibrant blue with streaks of red.

"There you are," Dad said as he saw me, "I'd like you to meet Miss Jane and Mr. Williams. They are going to help us in our studies."

Mr. Williams quickly grabbed my hand and shook it vigorously. "Sir, it's an *honor* to meet you!" Sir? I had to be *way* younger than him. He kept shaking my hand.

"I'm Mr. Williams, but you can just call me Greg." Greg gave one last shake of my hand before he finally let go.

"Pleasure to meet you, Greg." I rubbed my hand, some grip he had.

Miss Jane stood where she was and said in a quiet voice, "Angela Jane, Mr. Forjd, but you can just call me Angie."

I sat down in my chair. Mr. Forjd, she sounded just like House! I didn't say anything though, let them call me what they want, for now.

"Nice to meet you, Angie." They both sat down again. We each got our share of food and began to eat.

I soon became uncomfortable when I noticed that Greg and Angie wouldn't stop staring at me. Every time I looked at them they would quickly look away and stuff their faces with food.

There wasn't much chitchat going on so I decided to start some.

"So, y'all live in Alaska?" I asked at random.

Greg was first to answer. "All my life. Never been outa the state. Anything you need to know about Alaska," he pointed at himself, "I'm your guy."

"What about you Angie?"

"My family moved here from Michigan when I was four, been here ever since."

"Where in Michigan did you live?" Dad piped in.

"Lansing."

"I visited there once, is the old Eleven Eleven restaurant still there?"

"Ummm..." she faltered. She clearly had no idea what he was talking about.

"Dad, she was four."

"Oh yeah, that's right. I'm just so used to Kieth-"

"Dad," I mumbled; I knew where this was headed.

He ignored me, "And how he remembers everything."

"Dad," I said a little louder.

"What?" he looked at me.

I gave my head a little shake. Don't do it.

He knew what I was trying to say.

"Oh come on Kieth, you know I have to show off for our guests."

"Show off what?" asked Greg.

"My son of course!" He stood up and started collecting the dirty dishes.

I sighed, burying my head in my hands. Not again. He did this every time we had guests. I should have expected it.

He came to my plate last. I looked up at him and whispered, "Why do you torture me so?"

He stuck out his tongue playfully. "Go to your room."

I unwillingly got up from my chair and went to my room. It wasn't a punishment but part of a 'game' we were playing. It was a 'see what the difference is' game. So that when they called me back into the kitchen I would have to tell them what the differences are.

A few minutes later Dad called me back into the kitchen.

As I entered I noticed the differences right away but I didn't tell them yet. No one knew I was so quick and I wasn't about to let them know that.

They all sat around the table, in different spots than before. Angie had her coat on. The salt and pepper had moved, and switched places.

I stood at the end of the table. They all stared at me, waiting. "All right, tell us what the differences are Kieth."

Sighing, I quickly pointed at each thing as I said it, "The salt and pepper have moved as well as have switched places, you have your coat on, and your all sitting opposite the seat you were at when I left."

They all started applauding.

I gestured at Greg, "and your sitting in my seat." I didn't mean for him to, but he quickly got up and sat down in another chair.

Usually I would go to bed right after dinner, because Mr. Newark and Dad were pretty boring. They just went into the lab and let me be, but tonight we had guests. So I sat down, figuring it would be rude to leave.

"Wow, you're amazing!" Greg said, "I wish I could be like you."

"Uh, thanks." I didn't exactly know how to reply to this; I had never met anyone quite like him before.

"You think that's amazing," Mr. Newark chipped in, "You should have seen him do a maze blindfolded!"

From then on I kinda just zoned out of the conversation, I gave an occasional yes or no to a question but that was it. I chose instead to stare through the window and out onto the dimly lit porch.

I watched as a group of birds surrounded the bird feeder that we had put out there.

There were so many birds; big ones, small ones, two of the same kind, some with large wings, some with tiny wings, brown birds, colorful birds, and one curious looking lark with green eyes.

I got up very quickly, interrupting the conversation, and dashed over to the window. Most of the birds flew off at my sight, but not the green eyed one, it just stared back at me.

I stood there for what seemed the longest time, the bird and I having a staring contest. It eventually looked at me with its two green eyes and opened its beak. I had the weirdest feeling that it was smiling at me.

The bird finally flew off. But I didn't move. I watched the bird feeder for a while longer. I heard something behind me, but I paid it no attention, I was too concerned about what had just happened.

"Nevio!" I turned around. Dad had an annoyed look on his face.

"Wh-what did you just say?"

"I just asked you a bazillion times what you were looking at."

"No, no, no… what was it you just call me."

"I didn't call you anything, I just said your name."

I let the subject die, I knew he wasn't telling me the truth, but I didn't want to get into an argument with Angie and Greg standing there.

"Now, what were you staring at?" I didn't answer, my thoughts where elsewhere.

"Kieth! Answer me!"

"Huh? Oh, yeah. I-I just thought I saw something. That's all. It was nothing."

No one said anything, but finally Dad spoke, "Time to go to bed."

Finally! I headed off to my room.

"Hold on just a moment there, did I mention that you're sleeping on the couch tonight?"

"No, why?"

"Greg and Angie are staying with us until we can make way for Barrow."

"Wait, what about Barrow?"

Dad sighed, "Did you not pay attention to anything we were talking about?"

"Uh...." I had no answer.

"This Friday we are going to Barrow to continue

our studies."

"Oh yeah, right." Driving, I hope.

"So Greg's taking your room."

"Dr. Forjd, he doesn't have to do that. I can sleep on the-"

"No, I'll sleep on the couch, I don't mind." I left before anyone else could say anything.

I got my PJs on, grabbed a warm blanket, a pillow and my dream journal (didn't want any curious eyes looking at my stuff) then plopped myself down onto the TV room's couch. I didn't even bother to say goodnight to anyone.

I lay there long into the night thinking about what had transpired that day. First there was Fauna, running away from me, all the questions that were asked, then telling me to meet her for lunch. I guess I'd figure out what her deal was tomorrow.

Second, there were the unexpected houseguests. Although that was kind of expected, Dad needed helpers, and I guess these two were it, though they did seem kind of strange.

Then the green-eyed lark, I shivered as I remember the look on its face. Had it been smiling?

But the thing that bothered me most was what Dad had said.

Nevio, I knew that name.

It bothered me even more to know that he had tried to cover it up.

Why?

It bothered me so much that I got up off the couch and went to his room. The lights were still on, even though it was late in the night. I knocked, and heard the bed creak as he got up and cracked the door open.

"Kieth?" he said surprised putting his hand behind his back. I got a glimpse of that book that I had picked up in his lab but that was another question for later.

"What are you still doing up?"

"Thinking."

"About what?" he asked suspiciously.

"About what you said." I paused.

Then the questions flowed, "Why did you call me that? What does it mean? How come I've heard it before?"

He put a hand up to stop me.

"Some things," he said, "are better left kept a secret."

I became confused. "Why?"

"They just are."

"Well," I said flustered, "secrets lead to questions, and questions lead to answers."

He said nothing as I stormed off back to my couch. Eventually I fell into an uneasy sleep.

That night I dreamed of Blanket, she was running, from what I did not know. She kept running with such speed. The image changed. Blanket turned into the green-eyed lark. It flapped its wings ferociously, seemingly trying to get away from its unknown predator. The image changed once more, the lark turned into Fauna. She ran, and ran; but she began to slow down as it had caught up to her. The last thing I saw was Dad bearing down on her.

I opened my eyes and jumped up in fright. Something was breathing down my neck. I stood and got into a defensive stance, arms up at the ready.

As my eyes adjusted to the dimly lit room I let them drop to my side. For there, leaning over the edge of the couch, was Greg.

"What are you doing?" I whispered, "You almost gave me a heart attack!"

"Your Dad wanted me to get you up," he said, "breakfast is ready, sir."

"What by breathing down my neck? And stop calling me 'sir', just call me Kieth." I realized my tone was a bit harsh so I added "Sir."

"Sorry, Kiethster. I didn't mean to scare you." Kiethster? Well at least he wasn't calling me just plain old 'sir'.

"It's okay, you just startled me, that's all." I sat down on the couch. "Tell him I'll be there in a few minutes."

When he left the room I grabbed my journal from under my pillow, where I had hid it last night, and wrote down my dream.

After describing the dream in full detail I added at the end.

~ What this all means I don't know... but I know

it all means something. It must be connected somehow... ~

I closed the journal shut then rested my aching head in my hands. Why me?

I came out into the kitchen a few minutes later fully dressed and ready to go. I had tucked my journal into my jacket so I could take it with me. I didn't know why but I felt like I should show Fauna the dream.

I gulped down breakfast, and quickly left the house and rode on towards town.

I eagerly waited for lunchtime. I slowly rode around Main Street on my bike watching for any signs of her.

Some of my questions might finally be answered.

Lunchtime finally came... and went; I became frantic. Where was she? Had she been lying to me? A lot of people seemed to have been doing that lately.

Something touched my shoulder, I jerked my head around, and there she was.

I was about to say 'where have you been?' but she interrupted me, "Come on, follow me."

I didn't hesitate; I followed her lead. We stopped at some fast food restaurant and ordered a to-go then went to the school playground to eat.

Neither of us said much yet, we just ate our food in silence.

After we finished Fauna took our trash and threw

it away, when she came back she sat down and said,

"So, I agreed to answer your questions. What is it you'd like to know?"

"Well," I hesitated, I didn't know how to start. "First of all, why are you here? I mean, why did you follow me to Alaska?"

She inhaled and gave me a funny look, "I have my reasons."

I crossed my arms, "That's not answering my question."

"I know. But it's difficult to explain."

"Well go ahead and explain, I have all day."

"You'll probably think I'm crazy."

"I think *I'll* go crazy if I don't get any answers soon."

She thought for a moment, "Maybe it would be better if you answer my question first. It might help me to answer yours. So, how *do* you know who I am?"

I grabbed my journal from within my jacket and set it down into her lap, "I have a feeling you already know the answer."

She picked up the journal and flipped it open to the page I had marked while waiting for her. I needed to know if she knew what it might all mean. She kept reading until she got to the most recent entry.

"I didn't think you actually existed until you ran me over in the airport. What do you think they all could mean?"

She gazed into the pages of my journal. Not

answering. Was it just me, or were there tears forming in her eyes?

"Are you okay?"

She looked at me and sighed, "Yes, I'm fine. It's just; he took me. He took me and forced me to change, forced me to stay the same."

I had no idea what she was talking about. But she continued anyway like I was supposed to know what she was trying to say.

"I knew I had to get away from him, I eventually did. But I never left; I knew I had to keep an eye on you. I couldn't just let you be taken again."

"Wait! Stop!" I interrupted, "What do you mean 'again'? And what are you even talking about?"

"Your dreams aren't what they first appear to be, are they?"

"What!?" She was totally off subject, "Okay, all right. Let's start over, how bout we? Why are you here?"

"To protect you."

Okay, now we were getting somewhere, "From what?"

"From him."

"Can you specify who 'he' is?"

This conversation was annoying me. Why can't people just answer a simple question?

"Our uncle."

"What are you talking about? I don't have an uncle."

"How can you *not* remember?" she whispered, a tear leaving a streak on her cheek.

"What do you mean? I remember everything."

"Apparently not."

"What *are* you talking about!?" I was beginning to think that she was crazy.

"I'm your sister Kieth!"

"No, no. You can't be. My mother died when I was born." Dad would've told me if I had had a sister.

"I'm eighteen Kieth," she said in a calming tone. I was anything but calm.

"But no, you can't be Dad would've told me-"

"He's lying. And our mother hasn't died. Neither has Dad."

"What?" I was just about ready to leave this nonsense conversation; I have no idea what made me stay though.

"He took you from us when I was five. I managed to escape his scientific grasp. I don't know what happened to Mom and Dad though. I spent the rest of my years searching for any signs of them. I thought all was for naught, until I finally managed to find you. I couldn't believe my eyes when I saw you! I was so happy, but you had no memory of me. You still don't, do you?"

I shook my head slowly. No memory whatsoever, "Dad never told me-"

Suddenly, without any warning, she reached up and pulled the hat off my head, revealing my red hair.

"He's not your dad! Don't you realize that you look nothing like him?" I reached out trying to get my hat back but she pulled away. "Your hair, your eyes, your face! You're nothing like your uncle Kieth; *our* uncle."

"Hey," a voice yelled, "Who are you?" I looked towards the source of the voice. It was a teacher.

Oh gosh! The children had been let out and I hadn't even noticed. And now my red hair was giving me away! I looked at Fauna, ready to yell at her for ratting me out, but she was gone, hat and all.

Now I had two choices in mind:

1) stay and talk to the teacher or

2) run for it.

I chose option number two.

I grabbed my journal from where it lay on the ground and ran towards my bike. On the way, I tripped and fell, got back up, and quickly mounted the bike. I sped down the road towards the house, not caring at the moment who recognized me.

All I wanted to do was to get away from this town. I rode as fast as my bike would take me. I didn't even notice the pain in my ankle till I had slowed to a stop in front of the house.

I gently got off the bike and slowly put weight on the foot. I sighed, it wasn't broken, probably sprained it when I fell.

I managed to limp into the house. No one was there. They must be out getting supplies.

I rummaged through the kitchen drawers looking for a plastic baggy. When I finally found one, I stuffed it full of ice, grabbed a towel, then limped over to the couch and lay down.

It was only the middle of the day but I was already tired, tired of people, tired of lies. But, even though I tried, I couldn't fall asleep, there was too much going through my head at the moment.

I thought of how Fauna claimed we were brother and sister. I refused to believe her. She had to be lying. She was probably just some crazy girl who wanted to spend time with the 'smartest kid in the world'. She was just making the story up. But what was all that nonsense about being 'trapped' and being 'unable to change'. I realized that when she said 'he' she must've been talking about Dad but it made no sense at all.

My head started spinning. I have to stop thinking about it. I turned on the television and changed it to the US news. There wasn't much going on, just a bunch of politics, weather, sports and stuff. They were talking about sports at the moment.

"In equestrian endurance this week," that caught my attention, "Kit Friesian has been forced to forfeit the competition due to an injury to her legs..."

I immediately called her phone, not hearing the rest of the news guy's words. I waited, but all I got was voice mail.

I left her a short message. I hoped she was all right.

I had had enough of this. First the dream, then

Fauna, and now Kit. Why couldn't I just have a normal day?

I picked up my journal and flipped through its many pages. My journal was old. I started using it when I had learned to write, which was when I was three. My dreams became more numerous as I got older. I had never thought much of them, till now.

I stopped at the last page; there was a folded piece of paper there... It was a note...

~ Truth can be found in his book, find it.
-F ~

When had Fauna had the time to slip a note in my journal? His book? The one he always had with him? The one in the lab...

Fine, challenge accepted.

I got up and slowly limped to the lab. I knocked on the door, just to make sure no one was there. No one answered, so I entered.

Things were different from the last time I was in here. Lots of stuff was missing from the tables, only a few papers were scattered here and there.

I didn't see it; maybe he took it with him. I kept looking. I finally found it under a stack of papers.

I almost was afraid to open it. I stuck my head out the door and looked out just to make absolutely sure no one was there.

Before opening it, I realized how little I knew about why exactly we were here in Alaska. Sure, we were looking for something, but what that something was I had no clue.

I was in shock when I actually saw the content of the pages. I flipped through them. Every single page was identical to what was in my dream journal. The only difference was that there were notes all around my words.

Why would Dad have an exact copy of my journal?

I turned to the last entry; the dream I had that morning. He had circled the words: Blanket, Green-eyed lark, and Fauna, and had drawn a line down towards my note at the bottom and circled the word 'connected'.

I turned to my dream of the little cottage with the bed. I haven't had this dream in a while (thankfully) but he seemed to find it interesting. There were lines and circles around most everything. A note on the side of the page said 'I'm certain we will find her here, it all leads to Barrow.'

The page before that had the first dream of Fauna. There were many notes here, but one caught my eye.

'I'm hoping he believes this to be only a nightmare, I don't think he's caught on that it's true yet. Have her contained, for now, let's hope it works... can't afford to loose him to her...'

"What?" I whispered, totally lost on what he was talking about.

Just then I heard the front door open. I quickly hid the book back under the pile of papers and rushed out of the room as fast as my legs could carry me.

I came into the hallway; everyone had just come in the door, hands full of groceries. "Need any help?" I asked.

"Kieth? I didn't expect you back so early," Dad said as he sat his pile down on the counter.

I shrugged, "I decided to come home early today."

I went over to the counter and started to help put the cold things in the fridge (except some chocolate milk, I poured myself a glass of that).

"Why are you limping?" Mr. Newark asked as he saw me limp over to the table to sit.

"Uh, I tripped and fell while I was in town, must've twisted my ankle. I think it's only sprained though."

Hearing this, Greg, who had just come back in from getting more groceries, said, "I'll get you some ice!"

He started for the ice machine.

"No need; I already have some on the couch." He went back to putting away groceries with Angie.

"So why were you coming out of the hallway when we came in?" Dad asked. He never missed a thing.

"I just came from the restroom." I lied. I still didn't know what to think about his 'book'.

"Why all the groceries?" I asked, trying to change the subject. "Aren't we leaving tomorrow?"

"Well, maybe." He had left something out when he told me we were going to Barrow; I could feel it.

"Well, 'maybe' what?" I asked, "I thought we were all leaving tomorrow." I was becoming more suspicious of his motives now more than ever.

"I did say that, didn't I?" he looked over at Mr. Newark who shook his head in agreement.

"Well Kieth, what's happening is that Nexryt and I are staying here for a few more days to get everything that we need and then we will fly to Barrow when we are done. But tomorrow you, Greg, and Angie will be boarding the train that will take you to Barrow, and you will be arriving there Saturday morning so you all can help those that are already there set up camp."

He looked at me as if this news might upset me. But I wasn't upset, I didn't mind riding the train with two people I hardly knew.

"Sounds good to me, just as long as I don't have to take a plane, I'm good."

He seemed relieved when I said this. Like I wouldn't agree to it, he knew I had serious acrophobia.

Once they all finished putting the groceries up they came and sat at the table with me. I guess they didn't have any lab things to do at the moment. I just continued to slowly drink my chocolate milk, distracted for a moment by the chocolaty taste.

"Kieth," I looked up at Dad while taking another sip, "I'll need you to get your stuff ready to go and by the table before you go to bed tonight. The same goes for Angie, and Greg, understood? I have to drop you guys off at 6:30 in the morning."

We all nodded in agreement.

There was a moment's silence as I thought about a question that had been bothering me even before we had left Texas. It was harassing my mind so I finally ask it,

"Dad, what exactly are we looking for?"

"Well," he seemed hesitant; "to put it simply, we are looking for a long lost artifact from a thousand or more years ago."

"Why?" I knew what he would say, but you can never be sure.

"Science is an ever expanding amount of knowledge," (Yep, I knew it) "and to expand this knowledge we must discover it and what better way than lost history?"

Now that I had finished my milk, I had no reason to stay at the table. So I got up and put my cup in the sink. Then I sat back down on the couch and put the ice back on my swollen ankle.

Dad called from the kitchen, "How long have you iced your ankle for?" I simply replied "A while."

"Well I think it's time to compress it. Remember the old saying 'R.I.C.E it'? 'R' stands for rest it and 'I' stands for ice it. Rest and ice it for at least two days, ice only needs-"

I cut him off and continued what he was saying "Ice only needs 20 minutes at a time every three to four hours. 'C' stands for compress it. Wrap it from the toes up; rewrap it if it turns blue. And 'E' stands for elevate it."

I raised my leg up above the couch so that everyone could see that it was now elevated. That gave everyone a giggle.

"Now, where are the Ace bandages?" I asked getting up.

"Oh, I know. Stay there." Angie said, which surprised me, since she didn't seem to talk very often. She rushed into the kitchen, went through a drawer, or two, and then came back with the bandages.

"Would you like me to put it on?" she asked, "I was a nurse at the ER before I came here."

"Sure, go ahead." I rolled up my jeans so she could wrap up my ankle, figuring she would probably do a better job than I.

"Did you just quit your job to come with us?" she was lightly touching my ankle, I winced as she hit a tender spot.

"No, I'm just taking a month or two off to come be the nurse. Then I will go back to the ER."

She finished touching my ankle and started to wrap it saying, "You're lucky, it's only a slight sprain. It should be healed up in a few days or so."

"Thanks." I said as she got up and sat back down at the table with the others who had all gotten a snack of some sorts.

I lay back into the cushions of the leather couch; it was very comfortable. Even though it was only three in the afternoon, I probably could have fallen asleep (I was tired enough), but my mind was buzzing around like a bee going flower to flower. It was going from one thought to another. It wouldn't let me stop thinking about that book, journal, or whatever it was.

I thought my head might explode if I thought about it too hard, so I got up and went off to my room to pack my things which didn't take long because I didn't have that much to pack.

I came back into the kitchen with my bags and set them next to the table where I then sat down beside Dad.

After sitting at the table for a few minutes listening to the grown-ups talking about random things I decided I would try to change the atmosphere.

"Hey," I interrupted, causing them to all look at me, "Let's play a game of Bluff."

"Okay Kieth, go get the cards." Dad said.

I went over to my bag, where I just happened to have a set, and brought it back to the table.

"Does everyone know how to play?" Mr. Newark shook his head no.

"Okay, well it's basically a game where you get to lie. We each get some cards and the object is to get rid of them all. But we have to lay our cards down in numerical order; ace first, king last."

I passed out all the cards to everyone.

"I'll go first." I glanced over my cards then grabbed two and lay them face down on the table, "Two aces."

No one accused me of lying, "Okay, now it's Greg's turn, you've got twos." He looked over his cards then set down four on top of my two. "Four twos." "Bluff!" I snapped turning over his cards to reveal three kings and one two.

"Ha-ha! You get the lot." I pushed all the cards that were in the middle towards him, he then added them to his playing cards.

It was Angie's turn now.

"One three."

"Four fours." Mr. Newark set his cards on the pile.

It was Dads turn.

"One five." He set it on the pile very slow like, stalling. I could tell when he was lying. He always seemed to do everything with care when he was lying.

"Bluff!" I said. He turned over his card, smiling. I was wrong. It was indeed one five. I was forced to take the pile myself.

"Don't always assume the obvious, Kieth." He smirked.

I ignored him as I set down my new cards.

"Three sixes."

We continued to play until hunger stopped us. After we had a light dinner we played again until Dad told us to all go to bed.

Once my teeth were all brushed I went into the TV room, wrapped myself up in the warm blankets (it had become very cold outside lately), and fell asleep. I didn't even allow myself to think about the day's events.

In my dream that night Dad and I were walking

through the old town. I could tell that most of the buildings were burnt. I turned towards Dad and pointed towards one of the buildings; a burnt sign on the front said 'Old Barrow Inn'. We entered this building. My dream then repeated itself from the last time, ending in the same spot, the room and the bed.

We left early that day, having to leave quickly to catch the train. We almost didn't make it in time because we had to uncover the car, which had been buried in a blanket of snow overnight. But we managed to arrive right on time.

We gave our luggage to the luggage car handlers then we went over to say our good byes to Dad (Mr. Newark had stayed at the house, in fact, he was probably still asleep).

Angie and Greg said their goodbyes and boarded the train. Dad looked me over then ruffled my hat, which I fixed right away.

He then gave me a grizzly hug. I tried pushing him away playfully but he just hugged me even tighter.

"Dad, stop." I wasn't in a real 'huggy' mood at the moment, what with my ankle still swollen, and in a compress, and my head still aching from that night's dream. Also I think I was coming down with a cold because my nose was stuffy.

The train whistled.

"Time to go," he said, "I'll see ya in a few days."

He gave me a real hug this time then let me go. I hopped onto the train and found my seat next to

Angie and Greg. I realized this would be one of the first times I was going somewhere without Dad. That was an odd feeling. Especially when the people I was with were people I had only just met.

Dad stood outside on the platform, waving goodbye; I waved back as the train pulled out of the station.

Destination Barrow.

Chapter 12
Powerful

I think I had more than a cold, cause as soon as we got an hour out of Anchorage I started coughing. I coughed so much that Angie handed me a cough drop.

"Thanks," I said popping it into my mouth.

"Anytime," she said.

I lay back in my seat and closed my eyes but just before I could shut them, I saw something that almost made me choke on my cough drop. I saw Blanket.

"Blanket!" Everyone looked at me like I was crazy. I realized I had just yelled quite loudly.

Greg asked, "You want me to go get you a blanket?"

"No, I'll go and get one myself." I quickly got up out of my seat and limped into the train's hallway to where I thought I had seen her, but when I got there I saw someone that I really did not want to see at the moment, Fauna.

As I turned around trying to walk away from her she grabbed my arm and pulled me into one of the first-class compartments; thankfully it was empty.

"What do you want from me this time?" I asked her, "And what are you doing on this train?"

Actually I kinda knew the answer to that question, but I asked it anyway.

She replied with a sneer, "Why should I tell you?" We had a long moment of silence.

Finally...

"Did you find it?"

I was reluctant to answer, "Yes."

"And?"

"And nothing! I still don't believe you."

I wanted to leave but she was standing in front of the only exit. I tried slipping past her but she blocked me, "Let me go will you? I have nothing more to say to you."

In fact, I had a million things to say to her, but I was not in the mood. "You do know I took karate, yes?"

She didn't seem surprised, "So?"

"So I *could* get you out of my way."

"But you and I both know that you won't."

Ugh, she was right. I wouldn't want to make a scene.

"Plus," she added, "you're physically unable to do much at the moment."

"And how would you know that I'm 'physically unable' to do what I have in mind?"

She glanced at my feet. "If you did what you have in mind you'd injure yourself even further."

She was right again.

Trapped, I sat down on the seat and put my head in my hands, "What more do you want from me?"

"Only what you saw in that book," she paused, "or should I say *journal*."

I looked at her, "How did you know?"

"He showed it to me when I was his prisoner."

I rolled my eyes; here we go again with that

nonsense. "Well if he showed it to you then you don't need me to tell you what I saw. You should already know."

She sighed, "I didn't actually see its content, Kieth! He managed to keep that to himself."

She rambled on. But I interrupted her before she could get too far.

"Fine!" I coughed, "I'll tell you. It was a copy of my journal, but it had notes in it. Almost, almost as if he was studying it."

Was he studying it? He did always seem to know more than he was letting on. But what would he want with my journal?

"Is he studying it?" I asked her. "Is all he's really doing is studying *me*?"

"There's more to it than meets the eye, brother." 'Brother', was it all really true? No. It can't be. It just can't.

"I have to go," I said, standing. "My companions will be wondering where I wandered off to."

She didn't block me as I passed through the doorway. But before I could actually get back to my seat she grabbed my shoulder, turned me around, and shoved something into my arms saying,

"A blanket, for the ride, to keep you safe and warm."

She then turned around and walked off.

I watched her as she disappeared through the doors that led to the next train car.

Why did our encounters always end up with me having more questions than I started with?

Sighing, I sat back down next to Greg and leaned my head against the window. When I looked out upon the moving landscape all I saw was white, everything was covered with snow.

I covered myself up with the blanket; it was very soft. I fell asleep without realizing it, but just before I drifted off my thoughts were of Kit and how she could be doing.

Why could I not ever have a dreamless sleep? This dream was actually good compared to my other ones.

~ There was Image, and on her bare back was Kit. They were riding their hearts out, determined to get to the finish line. They soared ahead of competition like a cheetah on a chase. I don't know how, but I got a glimpse of Kit as she rushed by. She looked different somehow, a good different. ~

I must have been sleeping for quite a while, because when I woke up everyone else was fast asleep. It had to be the middle of the night. I looked at my watch, which confirmed my suspicion.

I got up, intending on finding a bathroom. Something moved at my feet. I looked down and gave a sigh of relief. It was only a Baggie filled with water. Angie must've put ice on my ankle.

I picked it up so I could dump it out in the sink, once I found it. So I walked off in a random direction in search of one.

It actually wasn't that hard to find the restroom

because there was a sign (should've seen it before I started looking, as it was right in front of my nose).

After washing my hands, I splashed some of the cool water on my face; it felt refreshing, especially since I think I was running a fever.

After going to the restroom I stood in the hallway, it felt odd standing there, being one of the only ones awake. I didn't want to go back to my seat, so I decided to explore a little.

There wasn't really much to explore but I did manage to find the kitchen area. It was buffet so I grabbed a handful of little carrots. They were nice and crisp, making that crunching noise as I bit off half of it. I almost had the urge to say 'eh, what's up doc?' but I resisted.

I walked back towards my seat now, ready to sit down and watch something on my wristwatch. I was just passing the first-class compartments when I heard something give a long deep sigh. It made me stop in my tracks; I almost dropped the rest of my carrots on the floor.

I looked over to the compartment it had come from. The door was wide open and inside staring me in the eyes was Fauna.

Relieved I said to her, "Oh, it's only you." and walked off.

But she was blocking my way before I could go more than two steps.

"What do you want now Fauna?" I asked annoyed.

"I need to tell you something," she said quietly.

"Tell me what? Oh wait, let me guess, this train is really going to Hogwarts isn't it?"

I rolled my eyes and walked around her but she stopped me again.

"Just come here and listen to me." She was staring at me with a desperate look on her face. She seemed to really want to talk.

"Okay, fine. But not too long." I followed her into the compartment she had been in, the same one she pulled me into earlier.

I sat down on the chair opposite her, she looked nervous. "All right, what is it that you wanted to tell me?"

"Where do I start?" she whispered, more to herself than to me.

"At the beginning, I suppose."

"Okay, okay. Well first of all, there's something you need to know about me. My name, my full name, is Kalani Fauna Forjd."

Here we go again with the brother sister thing.

"And I, as well as you, are a part of a dying race."

"A dying race?" I questioned.

"Yes Kieth, a dying race."

"What do you mean? Humans aren't dying."

She needed a straight jacket...

"Kieth, you should've been told this long ago. But you," she took a deep breath, "you are a Powerful."

"A what?" I had heard what she said, but I just wanted to make sure my ears weren't deceiving me.

"A Powerful." She appeared relieved when this was said, like she had been forced to hold a hot potato forever and ever and was just now able to release it.

"I don't believe in fairy tales anymore. And you and I both know that's just what the Powerfuls are. They aren't real. I was raised to believe in science, of what I could see and touch, relying on reason to come to conclusions, not myths.

People have tried to prove Powerfuls exist before but they never could, never have..."

"And just what do you know about the 'fairy tale Powerfuls' oh science child?" She was holding something back; I knew it.

"I know that they each had a special ability, or 'power', hence their names and that they all supposedly disappeared after the 1800s civil war. And I also know that they have their own fairy tale book sold in stores in the fiction section."

She observed me for a moment with those green eyes of hers.

"You don't know that much it seems. I'm surprised that the Dr. Freako hasn't told you more about what he studies."

"What are you talking about?" I became offended. I could figure out who this 'Dr. Freako' was.

"He took you from us, to study your unique power."

I don't know what brought me to it but I asked, "And what power would that be?"

"To see into the future."

I thought now about all she had said and all that had happened since that rainy morning and all my dreams since. If what she was telling me was true-

Oh gosh, I was in a heap of trouble.

"I think I might be starting to put some of the puzzle pieces together." I paused, "Do you swear that all you have been telling me is absolutely true?"

"I swear by all I hold dear, Kieth, that all I have been telling you is the absolute truth." I looked her over up and down. She *was* telling the truth.

Reality hit me in the head like a bowling ball. I was being studied, every year at that lab, every day in my own home. Never had I realized it, I always thought it was normal to write in my journal. But now that I knew Dad had an exact copy of it in his grasp with notes written all over its contents... Was my whole life a lie, a scam?

"I-I think I'm beginning to believe you." I was being truthful, now that my eyes had been open.

"Finally!" She rejoiced wrapping her arms around me.

"Whoa there! I said 'beginning to believe'. You said you are a Powerful, prove it."

"Uh, that might not be a good idea. Not here anyways."

"And why is that?"

"Because I'm really not supposed to be here. I was almost caught, so I'm laying it low till I get off this stupid train."

I thought for a moment, "Don't Powerfuls have some kind of sign... Or something."

"Oh, you mean our mark."

"Uh sure," I was going off of what little I knew about Powerfuls, most of which I had gotten out of children's books.

She pulled up her left sleeve. "Each mark is unique to each person, they are all different. But they each define a Powerful."

She showed me her arm. In the middle of her arm were two marks. One looked like an Indian drawing of an eagle, with two 'S' shapes above and below its head. And the other looked like some strange writing I didn't understand. The mark was slightly lighter than her skin, but it was light enough that you could discern it from the rest of her skin, even in the dark room.

"What exactly is your power?" I wondered. She put her sleeve back down.

"I'm surprised you haven't guessed already. For I lived with you for quite a while before escaping into the woods."

I gave her a blank stare. "No guesses?" I said nothing. "Ah come on, take a guess."

"I'm in no mood for guessing at the moment, so just tell me."

"Fine. I'm Fauna, it means animal shifter."

"Excuse me?"

"An animal shifter," she said slowly, "I can change into any animal I desire at will. For instance, the snow white Great Pyrenees that happened to be in your possession till July, that was none other than yours truly."

I didn't say anything more. I just got up and walked away. "Hey wait! Where are you going?" She tried stopping me but I shook her off. "Stop! It's true Kieth! I promise I wasn't lying!"

I turned and faced her, "No, that isn't lying, that's insanity!"

Her face looked like it broke when she heard my words.

"I'm not insane. It's true and I can prove it as soon as we get off the train."

A memory came back to me.

"You were the lark, weren't you?"

"I told you I'd keep an eye on you."

"You're spying on me!"

"No, no! I'm spying on *him*."

"Would you stop that!"

"Stop what?"

"Stop talking about my Dad like that."

"But he's not your Dad."

"Whether or not he's my Dad, he still raised me. Even if he has been studying me and I still don't have proof that he is."

"Isn't your journal proof enough?"

"No."

"And why not?"

"I don't know." My voice had become hoarse, must be part of this cold I had caught. I turned away from her and walked down through the train.

"You're going the wrong way," she said.

"I know. But you were in my wa-" a sharp pain sliced through my head, I fell into the wall.

"Kieth!" Fauna caught me before I fell all the way onto the floor. The last thing I remembered was Fauna's worried face.

Chapter 13
Truth

~I must free her. Take her away to the safe house. There's no other way. ~

I awoke on a cot. I felt terribly sick. Most every part of my body ached. I breathed slowly through my mouth since my nose was all stuffed up. I felt as if I was roasting from the inside out.

I didn't get up but lay there shivering, despite the heat radiating from my body. Even though my mind was groggy I saw that I was in a large tent that had dressers in it and everything.

Someone came through the flap that was the door. It was Angie she carried a steaming bowl of soup.

I was about to ask her what had happened but she interrupted, "Shhh, don't speak, it can hurt your throat. Here is some soup, would you like some?"

I nodded my head, but stopped since it made the world spin.

She sat me up on some pillows then gave me a spoonful of the warm broth. The warmth seeped into my toes; it tasted wonderful.

As she fed me the broth she said, "You fainted on the train last night, some nice young lady found you and brought you to us. We arrived in Barrow early this morning and now we are at the camp. So the good news is your ankles all healed up, but the bad news is you came down with the flu. That'll get you out of the hard work for sure."

That's why my body ached so. I hated being sick, not being able to do anything useful. Angie left moments later mumbling something about having to go set up the main tent.

I would have loved to go outside and explore a bit but Angie had told me that I was to be bed ridden for a couple of days, and even after that I may still feel bad.

It was hard, not being allowed to speak for two days straight. I had to write everything down instead.

By Monday evening I began to feel a little better. Miss Belle, the cook, had just brought me some chicken broth (which seemed to be her specialty) when Dad came through the tent flap.

"Kieth, how are you?" he asked. He must've just arrived for he had a briefcase in his hand.

I got my white board thing Greg had found for me to write on and told him 'Angie has forbade me to speak. But I am better than I was.'

"That's good. I'm so sorry we weren't able to get here any sooner, we had to finish getting everything we needed."

I shrugged like saying to him 'that's okay.'

"Well I have to go help get things together. Tomorrow we are going on our first exploration. I'll check on you later."

With that he headed out the door. But before he could, I stopped him with a snap of my fingers.

"Yes?" he turned to look at me. I wrote on my

board. 'Can I come?'

"No," he said sternly. "You're still not well, but you can come after you feel better." He left it at that. No ifs, ands, or buts. Its not like I could argue at the moment.

So I lay there, not really thinking about anything. But instead just enjoying the silence, if you counted random loud noises outside as silence. I couldn't go to sleep since I wasn't tired enough.

A little coughing fit came over me; it made my lungs and throat hurt. I took a cough drop from my bedside table and sucked on it, which helped the coughing.

I decided then I needed to do something to keep my mind off of coughing. So I reached under my pillow and brought out my dream journal (which had been with me on the train).

I had this theory forming in my head. I had wondered how Dad had gotten a copy of my journal and now my guess was because of a technology known as 'the copycat'. It was banned from schools years ago because it had the capability to copy whatever was on another's paper.

It made sense then that it was what Dad was using. I decided against writing anything more in my journal because of this. I felt as if my journal had betrayed me. It was supposed to keep my writings a secret. But now all my dreams were in the hands of my Dad and if Fauna was right he was studying them.

Actually, that was kinda obvious, seeing as how

he had put notes next to most every single word.

I sighed, stuffing the journal back under the pillow.

If Fauna was right, my life was just a lie. I wouldn't know what to think about myself. It was like I was only a science experiment, made for someone else's purpose.

I prayed to God that it was all just that... a lie, a prank by some crazy women. She was probably being paid to lie to me. Most likely one of those crazy TV shows trying to trick celebrities and stuff. I was no celebrity.

My eyelids became heavy as the noises outside died and my blanket engulfed me in warmth. I remembered the words Fauna had told me on the train 'A blanket, for the ride, to keep you safe and warm.'

~ A young girl stood at the edge of a baby pen, waving her hands around, playing with the tiny baby that was trapped inside. The girl had light red hair and green eyes with some freckles on her face. The baby resembled the girl, although his hair was more flame red and his green eyes took in everything they looked at. The baby was no older than one.

The girl looked over to her mother, who was sitting nearby watching the two, and asked "Mama, can I lay with him? Keep him warm?" Her mother had obviously passed her red hair down to her children; her eyes though were hazel.

"Yes Fauna, you may, but remember not to smother him." Fauna backed away from the pen and closed her eyes, clearly concentrating. She then transformed into a beautiful white dog. The dog however kept the color of her eyes, for they were still green. In a flash of white the dog hopped into the baby pen with the child, whose face lit up at the sight of her. She lay down next to him, the baby grabbed and pulled her fur, but she didn't seem to mind, she looked perfectly content.

The baby closed his green eyes, hands full of fur, and spoke even though he was considered too young to speak, I said, "Snow Blanket." ~

I awoke that morning, head throbbing as usual, with one thought on my mind.

I have to find Fauna.

I managed to get up without the world turning on me. I put on my shoes and went outside in nothing but my pajamas to keep me warm, I regretted that later.

It was dark despite it being seven in the morning. The only light was the light radiating from some lamps lining the outside of the tents. There seemed to be at least twenty tents all pitched in a circle. There was one large tent in the middle like a bull's-eye.

Assuming that this was the main tent Angie and Greg had been talking about I headed towards it.

Snow crunched under my feet as I walked around to the other side of the tent where I found the entrance.

"Kieth?" said a surprised Angie as I came into the tent; there were many other people in there besides her, but no one I was looking for.

"What are you doing out of bed?" I looked at her, and pointed to my mouth. "Yes, you can speak now. What do you want?"

"Where's my Dad?" my voice was hoarse from not being used.

"He took some men to go explore the area a bit, they left over an hour ago."

I was starting to get odd stares probably because the people there hadn't seen me before and I was in my pajamas.

"I'm going to do a bit of exploring myself."

"Hold on now, your still sick."

"I'm fine, I promise; I feel tons better."

"Head on back to your tent, I'll bring you breakfast, then I'll decide whether or not you're better."

"Fine, knock before you enter please."

I then did as she said, well sorta. I 'headed' back towards my tent but I didn't actually enter it. I just stood outside the entrance looking for any unusual green-eyed animals that may possibly be lurking around in the shadows.

"I know you're here," I whispered into the darkness, nothing happened so I continued.

"I sincerely believe you," I confessed. "Please come out so we can talk."

Something moved to my left. I looked over there

and sure enough coming out from between two tents was a cat. Its fur was split between black and white, the bottom half was white and blended in with the snow, the top half was black which must have blended in with the shadows. Its eyes were green (no surprise there).

She sat down a few feet away from me, putting her shadow black tail over her snow-white paws.

We stared at each other for the longest time. I was about to say something but then she turned around and walked off in the direction she had come from. Before she disappeared in the shadows she looked back at me, winked her cat eye, and flicked her tail.

I took the gesture as an invitation to follow. Before doing so though, I looked around to make sure no one was there; then followed her lead.

She led me past the circle of tents and out into the pitch dark unknown. The only reason I didn't get lost out there was because Fauna would stop every now and then, look back at me, give a little 'mew', and then continue on.

I had no idea where she was taking me but I hoped we'd get there soon, I was freezing cold and tiny flakes of snow were starting to fall from the sky.

"H-how much f-further?" I asked her, our little walk had already taken us about five minutes away from the camp site.

She turned and looked at me, then scanned the immediate area with her sharp eyes.

She then closed her eyes in concentration (can cats even do that?) and only but a few moments later there standing before me was the real Fauna.

From what little I could see in the dark she still had her eyes closed and I could hear her breathing real hard.

"Are you okay?" I asked.

"Yeah, just an after effect I've had lately. Come on," she said as she recovered. "Not too much further."

A few minutes later we came upon a rise in the snow. Fauna disappeared through a hole that was in the hill and I soon followed.

The hole formed a small tunnel; I had to crawl on my hands and knees to get through it. The tunnel wasn't long, it opened up to a small-enough-to-sit-in dome.

Fauna turned on a small lantern and set it in the middle of the dome. The light of the lantern quickly warmed up the room.

"Why did you want to talk to me? I thought I was an 'insane liar'."

I winced, "I didn't mean that. I was confused, I didn't know what to believe."

"And now you miraculously believe all that I've said?"

"Yes."

"Why?"

"I had a dream last night. Actually, it wasn't really a dream." I told her of what had taken place in the vision. "It was more of a long lost memory, I just know it," I concluded.

She giggled, a tear rolled down her cheek and into her long brown hair, "I remember that day. Momma had brought us outside to play but she had to pen you up because you kept trying to wander off. She always said you were an explorer."

Her face grew grim. "That was only a few months before *he* came. You had just turned two."

"Why would he want to take me away?" This question had been bothering me. Now that I believed Fauna had been telling the truth about Dad (uncle, whatever) I still didn't know why things were the way they were.

"I think he was jealous of Dad. He was the older of the two after all, and after finding out that Dad was a Powerful... Well... That's some of my theory, I didn't really know about him, till he took you. Mom and Dad didn't speak about him often, and even if they did, heck, I was five when we were separated who knows what they said behind my back."

"What did you do after you lost them? And how do you know they're still alive?"

"He told me they were still alive, when he captured me that night before I met you."

She meant that night I had dreamed about Dad attacking her. It all made more sense now.

"As for what I did. I ran. I ran as far away as I could from him. I didn't stop until I knew I was far, far away from him. I ended up in the Colorado Mountains near Pikes Peak. I had passed out, because like I said, I didn't stop for nothing. A young boy, who happened to live nearby, found me and took me to his home where he and his family cared for me.

"I don't think I spoke a word for a long while. As it turned out, this family consisted of Powerfuls. The boy who found me was Akira, he's very logical and can figure out any problem. When I finally began to speak and told them what had happened they took me in as their own and that's where I've been ever since. But I always knew that one day I would come looking for you. I vowed I would find you no matter what it took."

She smiled at me. Her story had helped clear some things up but not all, "And here I am. But what now? Why are we here in Alaska? Why didn't you just reveal yourself back in Texas?"

"I actually couldn't reveal myself, like I said, I was 'stuck' as Blanket. I don't really know how I managed to get 'unstuck', or why I was stuck in the first place, but I was able to change back to myself on The Fourth. I would have revealed myself to you after that but I found out that he had decided to leave right away so I really couldn't.

"And 'now'... Well, that's a little tough to explain. But I'm here because your here, your here because he's here, and he's here because..."

She paused.

"He's here because of whatever's in that old town, isn't he?" I said.

"That's our theory, yes."

"Who's 'our'?"

"Akira and I, well mostly Akira's, but we believe he has been using you to help him find it. And that he wants to study whatever he finds in there."

"How would Akira know all this?"

"He does *a lot* of research in his spare time."

I thought about what she'd said, pondering it all over in my mind. Trying to make everything fit together. Some pieces of the puzzle were still missing but I believed Fauna didn't have them.

Fauna interrupted my thoughts; "I hope you don't mind me asking, it's been on my mind for a while."

"What is it?"

"Kit."

"Oh." I felt a twinge of sadness. "What about her?"

"Her and Image are connected, how?"

"I'm not quite sure, that's the one thing I could never figure out about her. All I know is Dad was somehow involved."

"If he was involved it can't be good."

"No, it can't be."

I crossed my arms suddenly cold; I shivered uncontrollably. My flannel Scooby-Doo print pajamas (yes, Scooby-Doo was still popular) weren't keeping me warm enough.

"I probably ought to head on back. I've been gone too long. Angie will have noticed by now."

"You won't be able to make it back without me. You'd be lost in the darkness for days without end."

"Well let's hop to it then."

I headed out the tunnel first, I wanted to get back

before I fainted of exhaustion. I think I had pushed it a bit too far when had I decided to follow Fauna.

I was hardly able to breathe due to my stuffed up nose. My head still throbbed because of the dream I'd had. All in all I was still terribly sick.

I reached the end of the tunnel and stood up. That was a bad idea. The world spun underneath me, or was it above. I felt the frigid snow upon my face and seeing Fauna in front of me waving a hand in front of my eyes before seeing complete darkness.

Chapter 14
Historic Find

~Angie knocked on the pole of the tent; hearing no answer, she entered. With a clatter of silverware, the food tray she had been carrying fell to the ground and she ran for the large tent.

"He's gone!" she said to a fellow scientist.

"Who?" he asked.

"Kieth, Dr. Forjd's son. He's sick, I was supposed to keep an eye on him and now he's not in his tent. Holy crabs, we've gotta find him or Dr. Forjd will kill me!"

She kept rambling on but the scientist interrupted her, "Angie, calm down. We'll find him before they get back, don't you worry. Besides, he couldn't have gotten far if he's sick. I'll get some others to help search the tents."

He called out to the others that were in the room, "Go search the tents, we're missing Dr. Forjd's kid."

They all went out right away but they could not find the red head kid nor did they find any tracks on the ground due to a fresh layer of snow that had covered everything up.

Ten minutes passed in their searching people started to look worried. When Dr. Forjd and his team came back he didn't look too happy.

"I told you to keep him in the tent no matter what," he yelled at Angie. She looked at a loss for words.

"I-I'm sorry," she stuttered.

"Sorry won't bring him back now will it?"

"No."

"We must send out a search party to find him immediately. Put everything else on hold, because without him this expedition is hopeless."

He left Angie alone, then started barking out orders, "Greg! You take a group and start heading to the town of Barrow."

"Yes sir!" Greg and some of the other men got on some snowmobiles and drove off.

"Snoik, you go south, Trenty go east. Nexryt, you and I will go north."

With that they both got on a snow mobile and headed off towards the north, headlights lighting the way.

Not too long after they left, they came upon a hill with a hole in it and decided to investigate. Nexryt volunteered to go in first, though it was a tight fit for him.

"He's here! But he's unconscious," he called back at his companion, who sighed in relief.

"Pull him on out, let's take him back to camp before the real snow storm kicks in."

The snow falling from the sky was beginning to thicken and fall more frequently.

Nexryt came out feet first, dragging along an unconscious Kieth with him. Before either of them could pick up Kieth's limp body, a large white dog emerged from the tunnel and stood over him, bearing her teeth at the two men.

Nexryt cursed, "Is that..."

"Yes," Dr. Forjd answered, he then addressed the growling dog, "I wondered where you had gone. But I should've known you wouldn't have been too far away."

The dog just continued to growl.

"You can't keep this up forever. He's sick. And if you don't let us take him he'll eventually die in this tundra."

She looked down at Kieth, who coughed weakly, confirming what Dr. Forjd had said. With one last loathing glance she ran off into the white darkness, disappearing within its depths.

"Come on, let's get him back to camp."

Dr. Forjd placed Kieth on the snow mobile sitting behind him, making sure he couldn't fall, and then rode on back to the campsite. ~

I woke but didn't open my eyes; I was too warm and comfy to want to. After a moment or two I realized I was not the only one in the room and someone else had just entered.

"Wake up yet?" It was Mr. Newark.

"No," Dad said.

They were quite for a while. I got chills down my spine from the feeling of knowing they were watching me.

"Do you think she revealed herself to him?" Mr. Newark asked.

"She may have, but I can't be sure until he wakes up."

"And if she has, then what?"

"Then I'll have to wipe some of his memory, just like when I got him. Not a fun process, memory wiping, too unpredictable."

Wipe my memory!? Just like when he'd gotten me? Is that why I remembered none of what Fauna talked about? My memory had been wiped?

I wanted to yell at him, right then and there, about just how much I knew. But now wasn't the right time, my say in this matter would have to wait for just the right moment.

They both left, after the longest time of just sitting (or at least, I assumed they were sitting) and watching me, and I was able to relax some and think.

What should I do now? Should I leave, find Fauna and go live in the wild? Or should I stay here, lie my way out of getting my memory wiped, and find out what he's looking for?

I decided on option two; I don't think I could make it out in the wild, especially since I was still sick.

Right now I had to focus on getting better so I could go out on an expedition with him. I had a feeling I knew where to go.

But for now I needed sleep.

*****

It took about a week for my cold to pass. I still had a cough, but Angie said that was normal, and it wasn't nearly as bad as it was earlier.

They finally agreed I wasn't too sick to go on the expedition with them.

What wasn't better though were the intense headaches I'd gotten from the same stupid dream about the same stupid town with the same old bed. I had it every time I fell asleep. Every now and then I'd even have a daydream of it.

One thing was for sure though; I knew where we had to go. The dream was helpful in that way. The headaches sure didn't help my chances of going on the expeditions though. Every time I had an episode Dad asked me if I was dying.

I finally had to beg Dad to let me go one morning.

"Please let me go! I promise I won't be in the way."

He looked over at Angie, who was preparing a backpack filling it with water and snacks. "He's fine; he can go if you want him to."

"All right. You can come. But if you get sick again it's not my fault."

"Yes!" Finally a chance to see what he was looking for.

"Go get something warmer on, then meet us by the exit."

I was at the exit within minutes.

Only six of us were going. Dad, Mr. Newark, Greg, Angie, and some guy named Trenty were already on their snowmobiles waiting for me. I hopped on behind Dad and off we went.

We rode in darkness the only light around was

that of the headlights.

I knew the expedition was hopeless when the snowmobiles ran out of power.

"I told you to charge them!" Dad yelled at Trenty.

I was sitting on the end of our snowmobile twiddling my thumbs, trying to ignore the argument that was going on between the adults.

"I thought Greg did it!" Trenty yelled back.

"Hey! Don't get me into this, I thought Mr. Newark here was in charge of it."

They continued on like this, blaming one another for not charging the snowmobiles, for quite a while.

Finally having enough I interrupted them saying, "Hey! It doesn't matter!" They all looked at me suddenly remembering that I was there.

"Are we gonna get on with this expedition or what?" I asked eager to continue on foot if need be.

"Kieth's right," Dad said. "We need to continue to the place we intend to investigate. But we also need a means of transportation back."

He thought for a moment.

"We will split up into two groups of three. One group will go back and get the charger the other will continue on."

No one turned down the idea.

"Okay then, Angie, Greg and Kieth. You'll head back to the camp-"

"No! I wanna go with you. Please?"

He looked like he wanted to protest but instead

changed his mind. "Fine, Kieth and Angie will go with me."

"Why me sir?" Angie asked.

"Because you're the nurse," he replied simply, "The rest of you will go back to camp, get the chargers and then come and pick us up wherever we may be. Make sure and tell us when you're on your way so we can be ready."

We all grabbed our backpacks off the useless snowmobiles. We also put on snowshoes so we could walk better on the snow. Then we took our flashlights out of our bags, said a brief goodbye and headed our separate ways.

Was this really a good idea?

Angie, Dad, and I wandered aimlessly through the Alaskan wilderness for what seemed like forever. I was beginning to feel the effects of the below freezing temperatures. Dad on the other hand didn't seem to be effected by the cold, probably because he was too excited. He was holding what looked like a GPS.

"This way! It's gotta be around here somewhere," he mumbled.

I would have suggested that we stop so we could get some warmth back into our bodies but I knew better than to mess with Dad when he was on a role. Besides I was starting to recognize the landscape.

We walked up a steep hill, slipping and sliding in the ankle high snow. At the top we stopped.

I could have been dreaming again, for there it

was the town from my dreams, not a log out of place.

It was still dark but I could see the faint outline of the old town. "Holy crabs," Angie gasped.

"Exactly," Dad agreed.

We all stood on top of the hill for the longest time staring down at the vacant town. I managed to find the old building I'd seen in the dream but I didn't say anything.

"Angie," Dad snapped out of his trance, "I need you to stay up here, set up the signal for the others."

"Yes sir." She got to work right away.

"Kieth, you come with me, you may look but do not touch."

We started down the hill at a brisk walk, Dad suddenly acting like he was years younger. As we got closer to the old town I noticed that most everything was frozen but underneath the frost everything had been burned.

I followed Dad through the town even though I knew where we needed to go. We entered some of the buildings being careful not to bring them down on top of us as we entered.

Dad was continually glancing at his GPS, which he seemed to be following around. "There!" he finally shouted, "It's there! Oh, just look at it!"

We were looking at the worst burnt building; there was hardly any walls left and only a patch or two of roof.

This was it. This was the building. This was the point where dream met reality.

We carefully entered through the door-less doorway. Inside the building (if you could call it that) every surface was covered with frozen ashes.

"Let's split up Kieth, I'll take this way and you can go that way." Not waiting for me to answer he headed off into what may have once been a kitchen.

I took a deep breath, knowing exactly where I had to go, understanding that this was meant to be; no trying to stop it now.

Down the hall, third door to the left, and into the bedroom. There it was, the bed covered in a snowy blanket.

I reluctantly moved towards it and began to uncover the snow. The cold of the snow seemed to seep through my gloves, and I could feel a cold sweat on my hands. I tried to stay calm, not sure of exactly what I'd see, but I knew this was the reason we came to Alaska. I tried staying calm as I started to reveal the wood of the bed.

As I removed the last of the snow from the head of the bed I screamed out in terror as well as pain.

Pain because it felt as though a bolt of lightning went through my head, and terror... because; there was a body in the bed.

"Kieth, Kieth!" I heard Dad yell from the other side of the building. I didn't answer, too shocked to speak. Loud footsteps ran in my direction.

"Are you okay?" Dad asked as he entered the room.

All I could do was nod and point, still in shock, as Dad cautiously approached the bed.

"It's a girl," he said. I could tell that he was trying to make it sound as if he were surprised.

Before I could approach the bed Angie came bursting into the room.

"What's wrong? I heard screaming." She gave a little shriek herself when she saw the girl lying in the bed.

The girl had the blondest hair I'd ever seen; it could have been as white as the snow around her if not for the slightest golden tint. Her clothes were tattered and very old fashion. And on her arm was a mark very much like Fauna's but it was different. It looked like a stream with water coming out both sides of it. And the strange markings were different too.

It was a mark of a Powerful. "Nixie," I mumbled to myself.

"What?" Dad asked.

"Nothing," I said as quickly as I could. So this is what he wanted, this girl, I was sure of it.

"She's alive!" Angie said after checking her pulse. Dad didn't say anything. He must be thinking.

I stared at Nixie, a sudden desire to slap her face to see if she would wake overtook me but I did not, knowing it wouldn't work.

"All right," Dad said, coming out of his thoughts, "Angie, I need you to phone Nexryt, see where they are. Kieth and I will get the girl and will be at the hill in a moment."

She left already dialing Mr. Newark.

"How is she still alive?" I asked as we lifted her

carefully off the bed and out into the hallway.

"Kieth, there are many things in this world that no one, not even scientists, will ever be able to explain. She is one of them."

"Mr. Newark and the others have just made it back to camp," Angie told us as we got to the hill.

"Fiddle sticks," Dad said, we laid Nixie on the snow. I would have thought her dead if not for the slow movement of her chest.

"We might as well get walking. We'll just freeze if we just stand here waiting. Besides by the time they get to the snowmobiles and can get them charged we will be there."

I pulled my hat over my ears and tightened my scarf, ready for another hike through the snow.

Dad carried Nixie first. He soon got tired though half an hour later. He offered to carry my backpack if I'd carry the girl. I agreed, taking off my backpack. I then carefully took Nixie from Dad and slung her across my shoulders; she was surprisingly light.

I ended up carrying her until we finally spotted the rest of our group an hour and a half later. They had just finished charging the snowmobiles that were dead.

They were astounded at the sight of Nixie and the fact that she was alive.

"Who knows how long she has been there!" one said, staring at Nixie who was now on one of the snowmobiles.

"Exactly why we have to run tests on her," Dad

murmured with a glance at me. I said nothing.

Under normal circumstances I would have protested or something, but right now I was in no mood to do so.

My head was in a lot of pain now. Earlier today, it didn't seem any worse than normal, getting better throughout the day, but once we found Nixie, it started getting a lot worse.

As I got onto my snowmobile I shuddered as I suddenly had a simultaneous flash of hot and cold run swiftly throughout my entire body. This continued as we headed off towards camp. It took some concentration to drive the snowmobile while shivering uncontrollably and trying to keep an eye on the snowmobile with Nixie's limp body on it.

I felt strangely responsible for whatever might happen to her.

I was relieved when the campsite came into view what seemed like hours later. We parked right in front of the main tent. The guy who had Nixie with him picked her up and started to bring her inside the tent. I began to follow but as soon as I stood up I practically fell face forward into the snow. Well I would have if Dad hadn't caught me.

"Kieth!" he yelled supporting me with his hands, "Are you all right?" He glanced over at Angie who was soon by my side supporting me as well.

I slowly shook my head, "H-headache... C-cold... H-hot."

Angie felt of my forehead, "You should go and lay down Kieth, I think you have a fever."

"N-no, no." I tried protesting as they steered me towards my tent.

"Nixie," I said seeing her being brought into the main tent.

"Ross!" shouted Mr. Newark, "Ross, we need you so we can begin the tests!"

"Yes, yes I'm coming!" Dad shouted back. Then to Angie he said, "Make sure he stays here."

He left in a flash of canvas. I collapsed onto my cot, eyes tightly closed, the pain in my head almost unbearable.

All of a sudden the pain peaked to its highest, the highest it's ever been, and I was plunged into a past that was not my own.

~ It was the old town we had found Nixie in but this town was like a revised version of that town. The log houses were not burnt and there were some people outside enjoying the warm rays of sunlight.

And there she was, there was Nixie.

She seemed to be leading a small group of people down the street towards one of the busy areas of the town. They stood out among the town's people, obviously not from the area. Their clothes were worn from travel.

She stopped one of the towns-folk and asked him, "Where is the scholar of this town?"

The man pointed to one of the buildings then went on his way. She and her group headed in that direction.

"Nixie," one of her company said, "Are you sure

this is a good idea." I could tell there was a worried tone in his voice (for I couldn't see his face because he had a cloak on).

"Calm down Kavi," she answered as they approached the door of the building, "everything will be fine."

"If you say so."

She knocked on the door. A woman opened it.

"We are here to see the scholar," Nixie said.

The woman let them in. It was the same house that we had found Nixie in but now it was full of old books and scrolls. There was a man sitting at a desk writing by the light of an oil lamp.

"What is there I can do for my dear Princess," he said standing up and giving a little bow.

"First of all, tell us where the person we're looking for is."

"I assure you I do not know what you're talking about," said the scholar.

"I'm talking about the one my mother told me to find."

"And how is your dear mother might I ask?" This guy was starting to annoy Nixie.

The one called Kavi put a gloved hand on her shoulder.

"We won't be able to get anything out of him Nixie, we might as well leave."

She ignored him and continued on, "You've studied the stars and know the future as well as my mother did. Now tell me where I may find the one who may end the war with the humans!"

The scholar sighed then slowly said, "You may find him right here."

The scholar tipped over his oil lamp catching the floor on fire it quickly spread to the walls.

"What are you doing!?" Nixie shouted over the flames.

"You must understand they won't stop until your dead! I had to do it," he said desperately tears forming in the scholars eyes, "he threatened to kill my family!"

"Let's get out of here!" Kavi cried out grabbing Nixies hand. They all made it outside but as they looked around they found that all the rest of the buildings were on fire too.

"Look what I've done by coming here," Nixie said as she watched people fleeing their homes. Several children ran by them, carrying charred remnants of what appeared to be toys. Tears hung in their frightened eyes.

"It's not your fault Nixie." Kavi said.

"Let's get out of here," said another one of her companions.

"No." Nixie said putting authority into the word, "We must stay and put out the flames."

She gestured to a pile of snow then to the burning building behind them. The snow liquefied, rose up in the air, and then threw itself into the fire. It didn't do much to the fire but once she did the gesture again and again it put it out.

Her friends threw large snowballs into the fire which she then liquefied sending steam into the air.

In no time at all the fires were out and all the survivors had disappeared.

"What have I done?" she asked again.

"Exactly what you had to do." Kavi said.

"And now what? The scholar said they won't stop till I'm dead. They will kill everyone I know and love just to get to me. I can't let that happen."

Everyone was silent; the only sound was that of the cinders flying through the air.

"I have an idea," Kavi said.

"What would that be?" she asked.

"Well, it might sound ridiculous at first... But what if I 'killed' you?"

She looked taken aback at this, "and why would you want to do that? Just because one man tried to kill me doesn't mean you have to!"

"No, no. I wouldn't really kill you... Just, you know, fake it," he whispered the last part.

"Oh?" She looked worried now. "Do you think you can do it?" she whispered to him.

"Positive."

"What will happen of you can't?"

He grabbed her by the shoulders, "I wouldn't let anything happen to you Nixie." They embraced.

"I know, it's just last time-" He let go of her.

"Last time I didn't know what I was doing. I've been practicing on bugs and such and I'm sure I've got it down. They will see that you appear dead and will stop hunting us then we can continue our search and once we find the One the Queen told us to find we can free those who may have been enslaved. We will free them. Just like President Lincoln has helped free the blacks, we will free the Powerfuls."

She was silent for a long while.

"Okay," she finally said. "Let's do this."

They explained their plan to the others that were with them. They all agreed but it was grudgingly, they all seemed nervous about letting Kavi do what he intended to do.

Kavi and Nixie entered the now burnt building alone leaving their friends outside.

They found a still intact bedroom with a slightly smoldering bed in it. With a flick of her wrist Nixie extinguished the smolder with some water that appeared out of thin air.

"Okay, just tell me what to do," she said.

Kavi took off his hood revealing a head of flaming red hair. His eyes were most intriguing; they were completely white, absolutely colorless, with no pupils at all.

"Lay down on the bed." She did as he asked.

"Now just close your eyes and relax."

He took his gloves off then put his hands on each side of her temples closing his eyes in concentration.

"Kavi?" she said tiredly. Her breathing began to slow down.

"Hmm?" he was still concentrating hard sweat on his face.

"I love you." She said no more.

He let out a long sigh taking his hands off her

head, "I love you too." He kissed her cheek then sat down on the floor head in his hands.

His job was complete.

After a few minutes of sitting on the floor he got up and headed through the door but someone seized him and pinned him to the floor.

"That was easier than I first thought," said a man who just entered the room and headed toward the bed where Nixies lifeless body lay.

"What are you doing?" Kavi thrashed around trying to get away from his captors but there were too many.

The man did not answer. He examined Nixie closely.

After a moment he said, "She is dead."

The men with him cheered.

The man turned around and stared Kavi straight in the eyes.

"Take this *freak* and put him with the others, leave the girl though, let nature take care of her."

"No! No!" Kavi protested as the men struggled to drag him out of the room,

"Nixie!" The two men holding him suddenly fell to the ground having fallen asleep.

"Knock him out!" one of the men said.

Kavi ran over to Nixies bedside "I will be back for you. I promise!" he whispered before being hit on the back of the head with a stick.

He crumpled to the ground the men took him outside and tossed him in a covered wagon where the rest of his company were each inflicted with lumps and bruises. They were all in chains.

Before mounting their horses their captors set more torches on fire and tossed them back into the houses relighting them all.

They then got on their mounts and rode off towards the edge of the burning town leaving behind the sleeping Princess. ~

Chapter 15
Home Again

I opened my eyes. Something wasn't right. I wasn't lying in my cot; I was in a familiar looking chair in a familiar looking room. I looked out a small window and into the clouds above, below, and right in front of me.

My stomach did a back flip as I realized where I was.

"Oh peanut butter." I put a hand over my mouth and quickly shut the window. I took in deep calming breaths before my stomach could reach my mouth.

"I had hoped you would stay asleep till we landed but alas 'twas not true." I jumped in my seat; Mr. Newark was sitting right next to me.

"Why are we on a, on a -" I couldn't complete the sentence.

"On an airplane?" he finished for me.

I gulped, "Yes."

"We are on a flight back to Dallas. Your father decided we did not have the equipment needed to complete the tests on the girl."

"Where is she?" I asked, some of my queasiness was starting to go away.

"With your father, he went on ahead of us so he could go ahead and get started on the tests. I stayed behind to make sure everything was packed away properly." He mumbled something about 'people not knowing how to pack nowadays' but I ignored him. I cringed as we hit turbulence.

"Where are Angie and Greg?"

"We dropped them off in Anchorage, they told me to tell you good bye."

They left? And just when I was starting to get used to them. "How much flight do we have left?"

"Bout half an hour."

"Ugh." Half an hour of torture. "Tell me when we're safely on the ground."

I closed my eyes, trying not to think of how I was currently thousands of feet in the air. I thought instead of the dream. Did all that really happened? Was she really a princess?

Gosh, what had I been thrown into?

I heard the 'ding' indicating that we should make sure our seat belts were on and brace for landing.

I tightened my seatbelt then closed my eyes again as I felt the plane descending, my ears popping as the air pressure changed.

I relaxed as the plane was brought to a stop and docked to the main building. I asked Mr. Newark if there was anything I needed to carry. He just handed me my own bag and sent me off saying my father would be waiting for me outside.

I did as Mr. Newark said and sure enough there was Dad waiting for me outside of the airport.

"Up on your feet again I see," he said as he saw me.

"Yes." I didn't really want to talk about my fainting all over the place, "Where is sh-"

"Shhh," he interrupted, "Get in the car, I'm taking you home."

Home.

Kit was at home. Maybe I'd go see her. I missed her; we haven't spoken in a while.

I threw my bag into the back seat then hopped in the front with Dad. As the car drove us home everything around me looked so *normal.* All the buildings, roads, even the people, nothing had changed except the trees, they had changed colors, some had even lost their leaves. I realized that the date was November 1st. Time passed by so quickly and if you didn't keep up you would miss something big.

Driving into our garage, just like we had been only gone for a few hours, was weird. Nothing felt right. Nothing felt real.

I went upstairs and into my bedroom everything was exactly how I left it. Although (if possible) it was slightly cleaner.

"Welcome back Mr. Kieth, did you enjoy your trip?" asked House.

"Yes." It wasn't really the truth but I didn't know what else to say. I went back downstairs where Dad was getting something to drink in the kitchen. "So... Where is she?"

"She is undergoing tests as we speak in the lab. And to answer your next question, no you may not go and see her. She is still not awake anyway."

"Why can't I go and see her?" I protested. "I'm the one who found her, I deserve to know what's happening."

"I will give you a full detail report each night if

you wish but you cannot go see her."

"Fine... I'm going to see Kit now."

I headed for the elevator.

"Do not tell her about the girl, it is our little secret now. We cannot let word of her get out."

"I won't."

I had to fill my bike tires with air before I left. It didn't take long to make it to the familiar cattle guarded gate. I parked my bike then knocked on the door.

Mrs. Friesian answered. Her face lit up as she saw me.

"Kieth! When did you get back?"

"Just a few minutes ago actually. Where's Kit?"

Her face grew sad, "She's in the stables with Image. Did you hear what happened?"

"Yeah, sorta. Not much though. Is she okay?"

"Go on and see for yourself. She'll be happy to see you."

I headed to Image's stable and there she was just like her mom had said. She was sitting in a wheel chair, both legs bandaged up, petting Image's head. My heart tore in two as I realized how sad she must be. She couldn't ride with her legs like that.

Image saw me first but she must've told Kit for she turned around tears in her eyes. I ran up to her and gave her a hug she sobbed into my shoulder, "Shhh Kitty it's okay." I tried to comfort her.

She gave a little giggle as she started to calm down, "You smell funny."

I chuckled too, "I guess the Alaskan scent came

home with me."

I smiled at her. Finally, a familiar face, the one person in the world that I could tell anything to, bad or good, and she would still like me the same.

"What happened?" I asked her after a moment. I sat down on the fresh hay that was lying on the ground and started to pet Image behind her front leg.

She took a deep breath.

"A month or so after you left we went to a church rodeo thing. You know, watermelon seed spitting contest's, catch the ribbon off the calf tail. That kind of thing."

I nodded my head, remembering the one that I had gone to with her years ago.

"Well they had some bulls there and they were letting people ride them... Some of my friends bet me that I wouldn't be able to last for one second on a bull. I foolishly took the opportunity and tried my luck. When they let that bull go with me on top of it..."

She shuddered, "I woke up in the hospital; I couldn't feel my legs. They told me how lucky I was to be alive, how lucky I was that none of my organs were injured. The doctor said I might not be able to ride ever again."

Tears fell from her eyes again. Image put her muzzle in her face. Kit hugged her. I didn't know what to say. All I could do was sit there.

"You can't let this stop you," I managed to say.

She looked at me, "What?"

"You'll find a way around this I just know it. I have a feeling you'll be in next year's race I'm sure of it."

I was speaking the truth. She would find a way. She could make it to the top. She would make history.

"So how was your time in Alaska?" she asked after a while.

"Interesting."

"Interesting how? Be a bit more specific please."

I couldn't help it. I didn't care what Dad had said. "Do you promise you won't tell anyone what I'm about to tell you?"

"I promise."

I told her of everything that had happened in my months in Alaska. Everything from my headaches to getting the flu, and Fauna and Nixie, also about my supposed family I didn't know about.

"So according to Blanket, or Fauna; you're her sister, your Dad's not your Dad, but actually your uncle, and you're a Powerful with the power to see the future..."

"Pretty much. You don't have to believe me if you don't want to."

"Actually, I do believe you."

"You do?" I said shocked. After all, I took a month or so to finally consider what Fauna might be saying was true, Kit only took a second to believe me. I was still having trouble with it all.

"Yes, Image had said that Blanket thought differently than other dogs. I would never have guessed that your Dad isn't actually your Dad though."

"Me neither."

I still did not know how to believe in this truth. I didn't have much proof but what else can you believe when your dog turns out to be your sister and the girl you find in a snow blanket is Princess of the Powerfuls?

"What should I do?" I asked a little desperate for advice.

"I can't tell you what you should, or should not do but I think you should confront your 'dad', tell him what you know and demand some answers."

"I can't do that. Like I said he'll wipe my memory..."

She thought for a moment. "Well then, maybe you should find Fauna and ask her. She seems to be the expert on this subject."

"So glad I could make it back into the conversation."

I jumped up and turned around there leaning against the stall door was none other than Fauna herself.

"How'd you-"

"Hitched a ride on your airplane, flies can be very fast and invisible when needed."

Kit looked surprised at her sudden appearance but it didn't seem to faze Image much.

Fauna went over and shook Kit's hand, "Nice to officially meet you. I'm Fauna."

Kit didn't respond. I must've been the same way

when I had seen Fauna for the first time.

Fauna sat down next to me and said, "I think you should run away."

"What? Why would I do such a thing?"

"Because he's using you." she poked a finger in my chest, "Why do you think he took you on that expedition with him? He knew you could find what he was looking for."

"Nixie?"

"Yes."

"Why does he want her?"

She hesitated, "I actually don't have an answer to that question. See, I never knew what he was after I just knew that whatever it was couldn't be good. I never would have thought that the Princess was still alive. But why he wants her I've no clue. Akira might know though..."

"And what do you want me to do? Take her from his lab and run off-" she gave me that look like I was on the right track, "Oh no. No, no, no. No! I can't do that."

"And how come?"

"I just can't."

Fauna was about to say something but instead Kit whispered, "Hey you two! Could you keep down your bickering my parents will hear it eventually."

We had started to yell pretty loud. "Sorry Kitty." I lay down on the floor sighing, "I need some time to think."

Fauna got up and walked off but before she left

she said, "Better think fast before he pushes the tests too far on the Princess. She's not bound to last long."

"Amazing," Kit said, as she watched Fauna run off into some trees.

"What?" I asked.

"Nothing." After a few minutes of silence I decided it was time I left.

"Okay," Kit said as I gave her a good-bye hug.

"See you tomorrow?" she asked expectantly.

"I don't know... maybe." I walked off leaving her behind in the stable, "See ya later."

I walked my bike home that day; I wasn't in any hurry, I quite liked the walk, it gave me some time to clear my head. The frigid Texas weather was very enjoyable, even though my nose froze; it was better than Alaska's body-freezing temperatures.

Next thing I knew I was walking up to our garage/lab. I lay my bike aside, not really caring where I put it we really didn't have any neighbors down here. I looked up into the sky; I never would have thought that there was something above me it just looked like the regular blue sky. But hidden above some special 'concealing panels' was the large floating island of Upper Decatur.

'Stop thinking about it, you've lived here most your life with no problems just get in the stupid elevator...'

Something caught my eye.

I walked over to a door in the lab that was never shut. I tried opening it but it was locked, I made note of that. Must be keeping Nixie in there and doesn't want anyone to trespass unauthorized.

I went back up to my room and sat on the bed. Should I really run away? No. Why would you do that, you've got a good home and family... What family? Dad and… And who? I sighed...

I just can't steal the keys to the door, and run away with Nixie!

Nothing's impossible.

"Stop fighting with yourself Kieth, it won't get you anywhere," I scolded myself aloud.

I heard the door open downstairs.

"Kieth!" Dad yelled up the stairs, "Come down here."

"Yes?" I asked.

He looked frazzled who knows why, "Have you written in your dream journal lately?"

"No."

"Why?"

"I haven't had any dreams to write about." I lied.

"Are you sure?"

"Yes." I was starting to get worried. He was a bit too disappointed about this for me to be comfortable.

"Why do you want to know? You haven't looked at my journal for years." That was true in some sense; he hadn't asked to see the actual journal for quite a while... now I knew why.

"No reason, I was just wondering."

"Okay, well if that's all you wanted..."

Things were beginning to get awkward. I didn't

know what to say anymore. Actually I had nothing to say that could reveal what I felt inside, and I didn't want him to know how I knew more than I should.

"Are you okay Kieth?" he asked before I could head off to my bedroom, "You seem to have been a little 'off' in these past few months? Did Alaska change you?"

It sounded like he was joking but I said, "Yes, going to Alaska changed my life."

I awoke late that night. I had an odd feeling that something was going on in the lab and that I should go check it out. I quietly got up and went over to a panel on the wall. This panel was one that could control House. A screen came up asking for a code. I entered the code, knowing that this would temporarily shut down House's system. I didn't want her tattle tailing on me.

I went downstairs, keeping an eye out for anything suspicious. I was about to use the elevator but realized that would give me away so instead I used the stairs (which no one used at all).

The steps were creaky so I had to walk slowly down them in order to make as little noise as possible.

The light was on in the lab but no one was there. I headed over to the locked door someone was speaking on the other side.

The voices were muffled but I could tell it was Dad and Mr. Newark. I put my ear up to the door so I could hear better.

"Should we give her the Bionans to see if they will wake her up?" Mr. Newark asked.

Bionans... That name sounded familiar.

"No, not now. The technology might kill her and we need her alive."

"But what good is she if she doesn't wake up?"

"We can still study her, run tests on her, the usual."

They were silent for a while, though I heard the movement of paper and stuff.

Dad sighed, "What am I going to do about Kieth?"

"What about him?"

"He knows too much."

"Erase his memory." Mr. Newark said like he erased people's memories every day.

"I don't know about that anymore. He may find out. He'll know that something went missing. Why'd I have to take him from my brother? He's a handful!"

"Don't say that Ross. He's special. Who else can say 'I have a son that can see the future!' and then take over the world."

"But he's not my son. He's my magician of a brother's son." He said this with anger and hatred in his voice.

"Tell me again how you took Kieth from a household of Powerfuls?"

"Ambush, that's the only way to strategically get a Powerful. I had studied up on the history of the fall of the Powerfuls and apparently that's how they captured the remaining rebels of the 1800s. That's also the way that she apparently 'died'."

So he was surprised also that she was alive.

"I feel kinda bad that we had to erase the memories of those in Alaska." Mr. Newark said.

"It was necessary, we can't let word of this get out."

He wiped their memories! Why? It wasn't right. I had half a mind just to barge into the room and tell them what I thought about it. My fury was building.

"I wish I could figure out how to 'unlock' Kieth's futuristic sight just like I locked Fauna's ability to transform. That way I maybe could find out how to wake up the girl and take control of her powers too. His mind is just so complicated... I'll break the code someday though. But in the mean time I'll have to deal with what I've got. House?"

Oh shoot. I would have run off but they would hear me.

She didn't answer him.

"House?" he said a little louder.

Still no answer.

"Something's wrong." I heard movement come towards the door.

I tried moving out of its swinging zone but I was too slow; I got door slammed in the face.

"Kieth! What are you doing down here? You should be in bed!" he yelled at me.

I rubbed my forehead, tears were forming in my eyes, partly because of the sudden face slam and also because I couldn't hold it in any longer.

"You're using me!" I whispered.

"What are you talking abou-"

"You've lied to me! About, about everything!" I stood up, Mr. Newark stood in the doorway like he had just spotted someone committing a crime and didn't know what to do.

"You *are* studying me like a lab rat! Is that all I am to you Dr. Forjd? A lab rat?" He didn't make any intention of answering.

"That's what I thought!"

I didn't wait for any more replies I just ran past him and out the door. He tried stopping me but I was too fast for him. Ditching my bike I just ran as fast as I could away from the house and into the wooden areas, I knew where to go.

I knew that they hadn't followed me but I didn't stop until I saw the familiar outline of the old fort. I walked inside and grabbed some blankets that Kit and I had placed in there years ago.

I wrapped myself up in these, I was shivering uncontrollably; the weatherman had said it would get below freezing tonight.

I cuddled up in my blanket with warm tears streaming down my frozen cheeks. I rocked myself back and forth, in an effort to calm down.

I can't go back home. He'll take away my memory. No one messes with my mind. I cherished my memories too much; I couldn't bear to see them taken away. I'd be lost without them.

But I was already lost. I didn't know what to do. I didn't know how to get my lost memories back.

That lead me to the question, how much of my memories did he actually take? How could he do this to me? Why me? Why did I end up being his lab rat?

I sat there the rest of the night asking myself the same questions over and over again.

Not too long after sunrise I heard a rustling in the bushes. A moment later Fauna entered the Fort. She had some type of food in her hands. She set this down on the ground and gave me a hug.

"You were right," I said with a snuff, "I genuinely, truthfully, honestly believe every word you've said now."

She let go of me and looked me in the eye; her brown hair was pulled back and placed under a hat.

"You mean you didn't believe me before? I thought you said you did."

"I did and I didn't. I don't know. I think part of me believed you, while the other part believed that it couldn't possibly be true."

"And now you believe he's not your dad." I nodded my head in agreement. She picked up the food thingy and handed to me.

"Here, you must be hungry."

"What is it?" I asked not having seen anything like it before.

"Let's just say it's like a pop tart. Go on, you'll like it."

I took a bite of the thing; she was right, I did like it.

"So what's your plan now?" she asked after I had

eaten the last bit of my pop tart thing.

"I've been thinking about that and the only logical answer is to run away. But to where I don't know."

Fauna thought a moment, "I know where we can go. I'll take you with me back to where Akira lives."

"And I guess we ought to save Nixie from the lab?"

"Sounds reasonable."

"So it's a plan?"

"It's a plan."

She looked like she was ready for anything. I wished I could look that way.

We spent the rest of the day in that little cottage in the middle of the woods forming our plan of attack. Finally we came up with a suitable plan that just might work if done correctly.

I said that we should do it that night but Fauna insisted that I should get some sleep before we left. I couldn't fight with her.

When night finally fell over us we went to sleep, knowing that tomorrow would be a big day, the day we would kidnap the Princess.

Chapter 16
Glen Rose

When I awoke in the morning Fauna wasn't there but I knew where she had gone. She came back soon enough with some shopping bags in her arms.

"Gone to the store have we?" I said.

"And how did you find that out, huh? The bags in my arms?"

"Actually no. I dreamed about it."

"Oh," she tossed me one of the bags, "then I guess you already know what I've gotten you?"

"Thank you."

"You're welcome"

In the bag were some new jeans, and a long sleeve shirt, I went around back to change. Once I came back to where Fauna was she had us some pop tarts on a paper plate.

"Real pop tarts this time?"

"Yeah, they'll be cold but it's the best we got right now."

"No big deal." I grabbed my share of the pop tart and stuffed it in my mouth.

"Have any dreams about what'll happen?" Fauna asked.

"Nope," I said simply.

Before heading out, I found a pencil and paper in the Fort and wrote a small note to Kit hoping that one day she would be able to come out here again and read it.

We walked all the way to my house, Fauna

would have turned into a horse or something but decided instead to save her strength for our little kidnapping scheme.

When the familiar garage came into view we hid behind some bushes across the street. "Okay, remember what to do?" I asked her.

"Yep. You?" Was that a trick question?

"I never forget."

She was about to take off but I stopped her, "Intimidate but don't strike unless absolutely necessary. He may not be my dad but he still raised me."

"I know." With that she disappeared seemingly into thin air. But I knew the plan she had just turned herself into a fly that way she could sneak in the house unnoticed even by House herself.

I waited a full five minutes before I knew the time was right. I slowly crawled out of the cover of the bush and swiftly made my way across the vacant street. Even though I knew no one was there it still felt like the whole world was watching me cross that street and enter the garage.

The first thing I did, disabling House. The pass code had changed, but somehow I knew just the right numbers to enter.

After she was disabled I ran over to the door that had slammed my face the other night…

"Hello door we meet once again," I whispered, it was locked when I tried to open it "but this time, you'll leave with a bruise."

I got out a paper clip I had found and started

picking the lock. It was a tough thing to accomplish because the lock was programmed to change whenever it felt threatened, but I managed to do it, in under ten minutes (probably another World Record plaque right there).

I was off to a good start. Now for the girl. I entered the lab; it was just like I thought it would look, just like any other old lab.

Nixie was lying on a table like bed in the middle of the room. She had an I.V in her arm and an oxygen mask on, if I hadn't known the situation that I was in I would have thought she was a sick person.

I carefully took the I.V out of her arm, putting a Band-Aid over the spot where it came from, and took the oxygen mask off, knowing she would live without it.

I noticed she was not wearing the clothes that I had found her in, instead she was wearing one of the 'vacuum suits' (as I called it) the same kind of outfit that I had to wear when I was being tested.

I knew that the suit could be used to track us but for now there was nothing I could do. I just picked her up and carried her up the stairwell into the kitchen.

That's when I started to hear a commotion from Dad's room. I ignored it for now knowing it was Fauna 'distracting' him.

I left Nixie on the kitchen table and ran upstairs so that I could grab a few of my belongings. I quickly scanned the room for what I needed, and quickly tossed them into a backpack. When I turned to leave my room, I heard a loud crash downstairs

I rushed to the kitchen but he was already there holding a ferocious black cat by the scruff of her neck in one hand over Nixies lifeless body.

"Nice try Kieth but you'll have to do better than that to best me."

Fauna growled, hissed, and scratched at her captor but her claws did not reach their intended target.

"What will you do, now that you have me?" I asked challenging him, "You said it yourself, you cannot wipe my mind because I'll know it's missing. What will you do with me?"

"You won't know it's missing if everything's gone now will you." Darn, had me there.

"But I'll find out, someday, somehow and we will be in this same situation again. So what'll it be?"

I had no idea what I was betting on or even what I was doing I just knew I was stalling for some reason.

"I am going to lock you away so no one will be able to find yo-"

Just at that moment the growling of Fauna's cat died away but the hissing became ever more ferocious the black cat disappeared and Dr. Forjd nearly fainted when he realized what he was holding. He was holding a Black Mamba snake.

He let go of Fauna very quickly throwing her across the room. But just as quickly Fauna had him cornered.

She looked at me with one unblinking eye as if to say 'hurry it along please!' I grabbed Nixie and headed for the stairs that would take me back to the lower level but when I got to the door Mr. Newark was standing in my way.

"Going somewhere?"

I stumbled back up into the kitchen, knowing that with those stairs being the only way to get downstairs, I had to get past him.

Dad made a desperate attempt for freedom but Fauna kept him at bay.

"Change of plans," I whispered under my breath. I didn't know if she could hear me or not but I didn't stop to see if she was following. I made a run for the door that led outside in an attempt to escape. It worked, I made it but now I was stuck, stuck in Upper Decatur.

Before I could get very far I realized that Fauna had not followed me out. How stupid of me to leave her with the two men, even if she was a deadly snake.

I knew I had to go back and it's a good thing I did too.

Fauna was doing her best to keep Dad and Mr. Newark away from the door where I had left but they were gaining on her.

I needed a distraction but what to do? An idea occurred to me, I quickly went over to House's panel knowing Fauna couldn't keep them off for much longer without getting violent.

My hand moved swiftly over the panel's screen,

knowing exactly what I wanted. I finished with a smile playing on my lips; this would do the trick.

"Let's get out of here!" I yelled to Fauna.

I ran at Dad and Mr. Newark my goal being the elevator behind them. They grabbed at me (or more at Nixie) but their attention turned elsewhere as the houses fire system went berserk, right on cue.

Lights flashed, water poured from the ceiling soaking everything in sight.

The elevator doors opened just as I had told them to. I rushed inside letting go of Nixie in the process.

I then watched, as if in slow motion, Fauna make a slithering escape between Dad's legs. At the last moment though he reached down and grabbed her by the tail. It was a lucky grab but after that he wasn't so lucky, for quick as lightning Fauna bit his hand. After that Dad literally tossed Fauna into the elevator right before the doors closed.

I was too shocked to say anything. I just stared at the scaly thing that was Fauna not believing what I just saw her do.

The stopping of the elevator brought me out of shock. As the doors opened I picked up Nixie again and walked through the lab, Fauna right behind me. I went outside to where we kept the Ford. I put Nixie in the back seat then glared at the snake, holding out the keys that I had nabbed from the house.

"Change. I can't drive legally yet."

She did as I asked and then started up the truck.

Neither of us said anything as we headed off

down the road. We had already planned on a place to head for, so there wasn't any need to say a thing for a long while.

After a while I got tired of the silence so I unbuckled, climbed over the seat and sat down on the floor in the back of the truck.

"What are you doing?" Fauna asked.

"Checking on Nixie."

Nixie was lying across the back seats, exactly where I had left her. I felt of her forehead; it felt completely normal she was just asleep.

"How is she?" asked Fauna.

"Same. Still asleep. How do you suppose we wake her up?"

"I dunno. What do you think?"

"I'm not sure."

"Maybe we could... ah never mind. It's a stupid idea."

"Maybe what?"

"Well, you say she can control water, right?"

"Yeah. So what?" Get to the point already.

"What if we submerge her in water?" I pondered her words. "I know... It's stupid, isn't it?"

My mind jumped as I realized I hadn't replied yet. "No, it just might work."

"Really?" She looked in the rear view mirror at me.

"Yeah. Is there a water source nearby where we're gonna stop?"

"Yeah, we'll be right on the Paluxy. We aren't too far away from it now." I climbed back into the front seat, confident that our plan would work.

A few moments passed before Fauna said, "Kieth?"

"Yeah?"

"I'm sorry about what happened back at the house. I know you didn't want me to hurt him."

Way to ruin my spirits. "It's... it's okay."

"No it's not. You know what kind of snake I was. And I bit the man that raised you. I won't blame you if you're mad at me."

I took a deep breath, "I'm not mad at you cause it wasn't your fault." I stopped her, as she was about to say something.

"It's not your fault," I said firmly, "He caught you by surprise. That's it. I'm not worried about him any longer. I don't care what happens to him now."

"Are you sure?" "Positive."

I wasn't telling her the truth. I was just trying to make her feel better. I still cared about what happened to him but not in the same way as before. Things were different now.

"Good. Cause I didn't want to mention this earlier but that's probably why we aren't being followed by anyone right now."

"That and I locked them in the house."

"That too."

By the time we got to Glen Rose it was lunchtime so we went through a drive thru and got lunch to go.

"You know, if our goal is to go to your friend, who lives in Colorado might I add, why are we going south?"

"I told you we have to get across the Oklahoma border somehow. Technically I'm not supposed to be here. Actually, never mind; I was born in Texas. But that's not the point. I still have to get you and her across the border."

"How were you able to do it?"

She looked at me like I should know the answer by heart.

"You're seriously asking me that question right now?"

"Fine. I know, I know. Animals don't need passports."

"Unless you're a 'prissy poodle',"' she joked.

"Okay but you still haven't answered me."

"We're here because Andrew's here."

"Who's Andrew?"

"He's a friend of Akira and he can help us get across the border of Oklahoma."

This guy, Andrew, lived right on the Paluxy River. Like his back porch was literally floating on the river.

Andrew had brown hair, dark skin, and a fair smile. He seemed nice enough. He welcomed the sight of Fauna and I and invited us into his home. We gladly accepted his offer. Before entering his home though we had to get Nixie out of the truck.

"Sleepy traveler?" Andrew asked.

"You could say that," I said carrying her inside.

Once inside Fauna explained our situation. She

told him all about how I was her 'long lost brother' and how we came upon Nixie. I noticed, however, that she didn't mention that I could 'dream the future', which I thought was odd. She just told him that I could memorize anything in an instant (which *was* completely true).

"So, what do you say?" Fauna asked, "Will you help us?"

Andrew looked us over for a moment then gave us a big smile, "Of course I'll help."

Fauna gave a big sigh of relief, "You don't know how much this means to us."

The two of them then started talking details but I detached myself from the conversation, looking instead at Nixie who we had placed on a couch. So motionless. It was almost as if her clothes were suffocating her.

"Fauna!" I interrupted.

She looked at me in surprise. "What?"

"You have to change Nixie into something else. The clothes she's wearing can be tracked! Andrew, do you have anything we can change her into?"

"Yeah. My sister usually leaves spare clothes here. Hold on."

He got up and went into one of the rooms. He came out a moment later with some jeans and long sleeved shirt. They looked a little big but they would do.

Fauna went into the other room and came out a few minutes later 'vacuum suit' in hand.

I took it from her, went out the back door, onto

the floating porch and tossed the suit into the water. I watched as it floated down the river and disappear behind a bend.

Fauna and Andrew joined me on the deck.

"Are you ready to try our idea?" Fauna asked me.

"Not yet. Let's wait till it gets darker."

"You realize we have to leave as soon as possible, right?"

"Yes. But we can't leave till preparations are made, right?"

"True"

We all went back inside and sat down; Nixie was back on the couch in her new clothes.

"Okay, so here's the deal," Andrew started saying, "Tomorrow morning we can head for Pottsburro."

"Why Pottsburro?" Fauna asked. "Two words. Lake Texoma. I know a way we can get the three of you across unseen."

"Okay. But let's try and take a route as far away as possible from Alvord," I said.

"Trust me. We won't even be near it."

"Good." For once, I didn't feel like going home.

Once five o'clock came around we decided to have a quick dinner then we went outside where the sun had just set behind the horizon. There was just enough light to see what we were doing.

Nixie in my arms, I stepped into the frigid water of the river. Fauna followed me. Andrew waited on the deck towels at the ready.

"Flying Hawks! That's cold." Fauna said loudly as the water reached her waist.

"Hush!" I said trying to get her to shut her mouth so no one would hear us.

"Sorry," she whispered. Nixies feet and hands were already touching the water, which was waist deep

I lowered her down into the icy river, Fauna held one of her arms while I held the other. Luckily the current wasn't too strong because I don't see how Fauna and I could hold on to her with us both shivering uncontrollably if there was much of a current.

After several minutes of letting the water flow over Nixie, Fauna said,

"I d-don't think-k it's w-work-king."

She was right. Nixie was as lifeless as ever.

"You g-go on and g-get dry. I'll be t-there in a m-minute." I told her. I just had to stay and try a bit longer.

It was hard to explain exactly what happened next. There was a sharp pain in my head; it went away fairly quickly. But it left behind a name, a name I then used.

I bent down and whispered in Nixie's ear, "Wake up Laura Nixie Tarrant!"

Right as I said her full name she gasped, opening her eyes. I still had a hold of her, which was good since she would have floated off if I had let go. She stood in the water, her eyes searching, unfocused, all around her.

"Where-" she stopped as her eyes came upon me. A smile came upon her face and tears fell down her already wet cheeks.

"Kavi!" she exclaimed. She came at me, very fast, and gave me a kiss full on the lips.

Chapter 17
Nixie

After a brief second of pure shock I pushed her away, hoping with all my heart that Fauna and Andrew didn't see that.

"Kavi?"

"L-look." I said still shivering my tail off, "I'm, I'm not Kavi. But I'm not going to h-hurt you."

I offered my hand out to her but suddenly there was splashing behind me. It was Fauna. She looked as if she had just come out of shock.

"Gallivanting Hippos it worked! It really worked!"

"If you're not Kavi," Nixie said slowly, "then who are you?" She looked around again. "And where am I? And how did I get here?"

"I'm Kieth. This," I gestured at Fauna, who gave a little wave, "is my sister Fauna. We are both Powerfuls, like you." She seemed to relax a bit once I said that.

"We are currently in Glen Rose, Texas. And as far as how you got here, well, you may want to come inside with us because it's a long story."

I offered her my hand again; she hesitantly took it. We all carefully made our way back to the deck where Andrew gave each of us a warm towel; he looked a little shocked.

We went back inside once we stopped dripping, though I had noticed that Nixie had stopped dripping water almost as soon as we got out of the river. She was practically dry as we sat down on the couch with some hot cocoa.

I sipped on my cocoa not knowing how to start the conversation.

Apparently nobody else knew how to start the conversation either, for no one said a thing. I could only imagine what was going on in Nixie's mind at the moment.

I looked at her over the edge of my mug, she hadn't touched her cocoa yet, and instead she was looking around the room. Finally her eyes landed on me and they didn't move; she had an intimidating stare.

"Spill it," she said.

"What?" I said quickly looking at my mug, I hadn't spilled anything nor was I planning to.

"Tell me how I got here. And where are my friends?"

"I don't know where to begin..."

I took a deep breath then told her everything, from Texas, to Alaska, and back again. Though, like Fauna, I didn't tell her I had any peculiar dreams. I just told her I memorized everything. I didn't even tell her of the dream I had about her and her friends. Now just wasn't the time or place for that.

"So you see, our uncle wants to study us. That's why we went to Alaska. We were searching for you."

She was silent for a long while. I let her be. It was a lot to take in. "So you mean-" she hesitated then asked, "How long was I asleep?"

"Uh, what year did you go to that village in Alaska?"

"I think it was 1864."

"That means..." Fauna started.

"No way!" Andrew gasped.

"What?" Nixie said.

I had done the math in my head.

"It means," I sighed not wanting to be the person to tell her this, "It means your over one thousand one hundred years old."

"That's, that's not possible," she said stunned.

"Apparently it is." Andrew said stating the obvious.

"But, how?" she looked at me again, and I swear I saw her mouth the name 'Kavi'. Then there was an awkward silence between all of us.

"Well," Andrew sat up and clapped his hands, "We should probably go to bed; we'll have to get up early tomorrow morning."

"Right," Fauna agreed, "where can we sleep?"

"I only have one spare bedroom but I have plenty of blankets."

"I'll sleep on the couch," I offered, I really didn't care. "The girls can take the spare."

Fauna led Nixie into the other room. Andrew went off too but came back with an armful of blankets.

"Here ya go," he said handing them all to me. "Keep warm." Then he left, leaving me all to myself.

I lay down where I was, covering myself with

the blankets, I didn't even bother to go get my pajamas on.

I woke suddenly in the middle of the night. I was having another dream but that's not what woke me. It was the sound of the back door closing.

What was she doing?

I grabbed two of my blankets, and followed.

I quietly opened and closed the door.

"What are you doing?" I asked.

Nixie jumped around at the sound of my voice.

"What are *you* doing?" she asked.

"Seeing what you're doing out here in the middle of the night."

She sighed, "I couldn't sleep."

I chuckled, "I can understand why, seeing as how you slept for over a millennium."

She turned around and sat on the edge of the deck letting her feet dangle in the water and said, "Please don't remind me about that."

"I'm sorry, I didn't mean anything by it," I said quietly. I came up behind her and placed one of the blankets around her shoulders, I then sat crisscross beside her with my own blanket (I wasn't about to put my feet back in that ice cold water).

"The water, its different." she scooped up some water in her hands.

"How?" I asked; water was water.

"I'm not sure. It just is." She opened her hands but the water stayed where it was. After a moment it fell back into the river.

"Wow." I said. Having only seen her do the water

tricks in the memory I had of her, I was clearly amazed...

"What?"

"Nothing, I've just never seen anything like... that... before."

"That? That was nothing. Simple. You should have seen this one time I-" she stopped, stuck on her words. She pulled the blanket up higher seemingly to try and cover her face.

"What's wrong?" I asked.

She didn't answer. I could see tears falling down her cheeks.

"Are you okay Nixie?"

"They're all gone." she said after a moment, "All my friends are gone. I have no way of knowing if they were enslaved or not. Did they live to see a new day?"

I didn't know what to tell her, I couldn't just say they were captured because that would give away the fact that I knew more than I should so I lied.

"I don't know what became of your friends but that's why we have to go to Fauna's friend, he should know more about what happened."

"Do you think so?" She looked at me with sad blue eyes.

"Yeah, I'm pretty sure, he's supposed to be a smart guy."

She gave me a smile then turned her attention back to the water. We were both silent for a while, I had nothing to say any way.

"I'm sorry," she said.

"For what?" I asked confused.

"For earlier, I-I thought you were someone else."

"Oh," I couldn't blame her, apparently Kavi had red hair too but I couldn't say that.

"It's just you look so much like him. Everything except your eyes."

"What does Kavi mean? What was his ability?" I had a hunch but wasn't too sure.

"Kavi was his human name, his Powerful name was Lugono, which basically means 'sleep'. He was able to put anyone to sleep with just a touch or sometimes even a thought. He was misunderstood a lot; people thought he was odd. But if you got to know him a little, you find that there's more than meets the eye."

"I'm sorry; he sounded like a nice guy."

"Yes, he was."

There was now a question burning on my tongue that I had to ask, "What brought you to Alaska, Nixie?"

"'Hard times we face, we're all dying in this place. Imprisonment is sure to come if the one who sees all is not found.' That is the last prophecy my mother gave us."

"She could see the future?" I interrupted.

"Yes and no. She didn't really 'see' the future, she just told the future through words or poems. Most of her prophecies made no sense, even she admitted that at one time."

"So that's what you were doing in Alaska. Looking for 'the one who sees all'?"

"Yes."

"Did you find him?"

"No, that is why, as soon as I find out what happened to my companions, I must go. I must go and continue what I started."

"Why? There is nothing to fear anymore. No more enslavement of innocent people and no more wars. Everything is peaceful."

She looked at me hard in the eyes, eyes that had seen many troubling times I'm sure.

"Is it? Is it peaceful? As you told me, your uncle stole you away, took you in as a lab rat, and studied you. Earlier today, he attacked you in an attempt to keep you under lock and key. Is the world truly peaceful, Kieth?"

I stood up, taken aback at her harsh words. But what she said was true enough; the world *wasn't* at peace, at least, not my part of the world.

"No. It's not." I stood there for a little while longer I said nothing until I decided to leave.

"Good night." She didn't reply so I just left her there on the porch in the dark of the late night.

I lied back down on the couch under my bed of blankets, and fell back to sleep. Only to be rudely awakened a few hours later by Fauna who had actually turned into Blanket and was currently licking my face with her sopping wet tongue.

"Stop, stop! I'm awake, I'm up!" I tried pushing her off but that just resulted in she, and I, both rolling around on the floor in some kind of makeshift wrestling match.

After a few 'please get off me's' I was able to get up.

"Good morning," she said turning back into herself. I just gave her a forced smile and then used the blankets to wipe dog slobber off my face.

"Andrew's out getting things ready for us to go," she said heading off towards the kitchen.

"Where's Nixie?" I asked, my voice muffled through the blankets.

"She's washing up."

"Sounds like a good idea to me. I think I'm gonna change at least."

I went out to the truck to grab my bag. It was a nice day out. The leaves were falling, the air nice and crisp but not too cold. Better than the other day at least.

By the time I got done changing into fresh clothes everyone else was eating scrambled eggs.

"Smells good," I said.

"Tastes good too!" said Fauna through a mouthful of some bacon. So, I sat down and had my fill of eggs and bacon too.

Soon after eating we quickly packed up our things and piled into the truck. Andrew was given the job of driver; Fauna took shotgun and that left Nixie and I in the back.

Nixie seemed to go along with whatever happened after getting into the car, at first she had seemed a little nervous, and maybe even a little sickly but she soon got used to it.

A little ways out of Glen Rose I asked, "Andrew?

What's your 'power'?" He hadn't mentioned it so I might as well ask now rather than later.

"Well, uh..." He seemed reluctant to speak. "I can make people believe lies."

"Oh." It made sense now why Fauna had taken us to him, he could just lie our way across the border. But unfortunately I also understood why he would be reluctant to tell us what he could do; we probably wouldn't take him seriously anymore.

"Yeah, some great power I know," he said sarcastically but then he cheered up, "I've learned how to use it though and that's the important thing."

"Oh I hated it when I didn't have much control of my power! It was awful!" Fauna said, "Always, I was turning into something whenever I got mad or sad or even overly happy, it was horrible. One day I got really mad, this was when I was young and Kieth was just a baby, I don't remember why I got mad but I turned into a cat and just about clawed off Kieth's head."

I touched my neck, I liked my head.

"I would have too if my Mom hadn't stopped me."

~ A young red head girl holding a sopping wet doll suddenly turned into a small cat which came towards the little red head boy sitting in the mud, claws extended. But the little girl's mother who had been nearby stopped the cat. ~

This all flashed through my head as Andrew

laughed at what Fauna had said. "Let that be a reminder to all to not get on your bad side."

"I remember," I said real slowly, Fauna looked back at me, surprise on her face, "I remember I had dropped your favorite toy in the mud."

Recognition dawned on her face, "Yes! It was my favorite doll and I wasn't able to get that mud out of her hair for months! How did you remember? Dr. F destroyed those memories, didn't he?"

"Yeah, I guess so..." I didn't understand any of what was going on.

Fauna and Andrew asked me a few more questions about it but I just gave them blunt answers and they soon stopped trying. Nixie didn't say anything; instead she chose to freak me out by unblinkingly staring straight at me.

I was about to question her but decided against it. I instead looked out the window and took in the scenery. Buildings, trees, and signs flashed pass the window but I paid them no attention. What had just happened? I was kinda excited at the possibility of getting some of my memory back but it still confused me. Why did it happen? What triggered it? How could I trigger it again?

I guess I was like Fauna when she was little, still learning. I had to learn to control it, I didn't see how though... It's not like the future was a *physical* thing I could move around.

Why was I given this ability?

What was my purpose?

These questions were stuck in my head all the

way to Pottsburro. But I had no answer and there was no way I was about to ask anyone else.

Andrew drove off the highway and got onto some back roads, which we followed for a little ways until we came upon the place Andrew had been talking about.

Chapter 18
Through Camp Arrow

"Arrow Summer Camp?" I asked, reading the sign on the gate as we drove in the driveway.

"Yep, summer camp in the summer, getaway cabins the rest of the time." "And why are we here?" Nixie asked him.

"Because this is the best spot to get near the lake, plus I know the owner so that helps too."

We got out of the truck at the end of the road; this is where a bunch of cabins were. The cabins all had an old Native American look to them; they weren't teepees but had Indian paintings on them and stuff. There was also one large building off to the side. The sign on this building said 'food court'.

There were well-worn paths that lead past the cabins and worked their way towards the lake. Andrew led us down one of these paths. The path came out onto a little lake beach where a family was eating lunch.

I pulled my jacket hood over my head not wanting to be recognized. As we got closer one of them caught sight of us.

"Andrew!" he shouted as he saw Andrew.

"Hey, Sea Bison!" Andrew waved at the man. "How's it going?"

"Good! You?"

"Great!" They shook hands when we got closer.

"Who you got here?" the man asked gesturing at

Fauna, Nixie, and I.

"These are my friends." He introduced us and we each shook hands with him.

"Nice to meet you all and welcome to Arrow Camp. My names Charlie but everyone around here calls me Sea Bison. I'm the owner of this camp."

Sea Bison lead us over to where his family (I assumed) was eating. "Have y'all had lunch?" he asked. We shook our heads 'no'. "Well come join us! We just started."

We all ended up getting a PB&J sandwich made by Sea Bison's wife, Bandy. He also had two daughters, Nenal and Perl.

"So what brings you to Arrow Camp Andrew?" Sea Bison asked as we ate.

"I wanted to take my friends here boating. They're from southern Texas and are only visiting for a few days and I knew you'd let me borrow your boat."

"Of course, of course! I'll get the boat out after we eat."

An hour or so later we all got onto Sea Bison's decent sized motorized boat. I sat in the front of the boat with my back to the wind so my hood wouldn't come off with Nixie and Fauna who sat next to me. Nixie was doing real good with not asking any questions (which I'm sure she had plenty of) she seemed totally content as we sailed over the lake at 20 mph or more.

"So where in South Texas are y'all from?"

"Galveston," Fauna said automatically. Everyone knew where Galveston was.

"I here y'all get a lot of tropical storms down there?"

"Some but we're protected by the cities weather shield now. So there's no damage," I told him. I had read up on the weather shields a while back, they were real helpful.

"Ever been to the north side?" he asked pointing towards the Oklahoma border.

"I haven't. What about you?" Nixie said.

"Many times." After a minute or two of riding around, Andrew started patting his pockets.

"Aw darn it!" he threw his hands to his sides,

"Sea Bison? Can we go back to the shore? I forgot my camera and I wanted to take a picture of them on the boat."

"Sure thing." He turned the boat around and headed back to land.

Once back on solid ground, we followed Andrew to the car; Sea Bison stayed with the boat.

As we got near the car Fauna blurted out, "Okay Andrew, what's the plan? You have me confused. I thought we would be over the border by now, what's the deal?"

"You forgot your bags," he stated simply. Fauna blushed, "Oh, yeah... I knew that."

She tossed me my bag as she searched for her own. As she was trying to pull her bag out of the back I decided I'd get my hat out of my own bag, I had gotten tired of the hoodie. I put the blue beanie on my head.

Would I have to wear a hat for the rest of my life? To hide from people who might turn me in?

I slung my backpack over my shoulders just as Fauna had finally gotten hers unstuck. "Okay, let's do this," she said, shouldering her own backpack.

"All right," Andrew whispered, "Just remember that I really have no control over who my power effects."

"Ha-ha yeah. You almost made me believe I *was* from South Texas. I had to keep reminding myself that I wasn't." Fauna said.

"Yeah, well just keep doing that..." Andrew smiled weakly putting his thumbs up then walked off back towards the lake.

"I didn't experience that," I told Fauna.

"Hmm, maybe that's because you had a place to call your home. For a while anyways."

We followed Andrew back to the boat where we all got back on. I had an odd feeling that this was the last time I would set foot in Texas for a while. There was no turning back now.

Andrews plan took action somewhere in the middle of the lake. He started by taking pictures of us sitting together on the boat.

"Smile!" he would say, I gave him the best fake smile I could muster. After a minute of random picture taking he stopped obviously thinking about something. He then looked at Sea Bison.

"Hey Sea Bison," he said.

"Yeah?"

"I know this may sound crazy... But do you think you could get us onto Oklahoma soil so I can take a picture?"

Sea Bison looked taken aback a little. "Oklahoma soil? Do all of y'all have passports?"

"Of course they do!" He was still looking at Sea Bison but then looked at us as he said, "Don't y'all!"

I noticed Andrew flinch a little as we all said 'yes' in unison but Sea Bison didn't notice. I had a passport but I was pretty sure Fauna didn't have one and I was defiantly sure that Nixie didn't have one.

"Okay then, as long as you have your passports we can get onto Oklahoma soil." Sea Bison turned the boat towards Oklahoma.

Before we could get to the border we had to go through the 'Checkpoint', which was basically a bunch of docks on the border where security guards stood watch. It was almost like a tollbooth on water.

We slowly sailed up to the checkpoint. I was pretty nervous. I had my passport on me but I couldn't use it. I would be recognized right away, especially if a certain someone was searching for me... If he had survived...

As we pulled up the security guard raised his hand in greetings, "Sea Bison! Long time no see. What brings you to our side of the lake?"

Sea Bison pulled out his passport and handed it to the guard, "These kids wanna take a picture on y'all's beaches. They're from down South Texas."

"Hope you all have your passports, wouldn't want to have to turn you all aw," the guard said handing Sea Bison back his passport.

Andrew looked at the guy and held out his hand like he was holding something, "Here, they put me in charge of their passports, not wanting to lose them in the water was their excuse."

The guard reached out and apparently took whatever Andrew seemed to be offering him. But then I realized that he was looking over our passports. I shook my head trying to get rid of the illusion.

"Everything checks out." He handed the fake passports back to Andrew where they seemed to disappear but no one noticed.

We were given the green light and we passed on through. Andrew seemed to relax a little as we got to the Oklahoma beach.

Sea Bison shut off the boat, "Go on, and take your first pictures in America. I'll wait here."

We all hopped off onto the sand and walked several feet away from the boat.

Andrew took out his camera and snapped away.

Fauna and I 'fake posed' for the benefit of curious eyes.

"This is where I leave y'all," Andrew said as he 'showed' us the pictures.

"Thank you, Andrew." Fauna said.

"Always glad to help." He smiled back. "Be sure to tell Akira that I said hi!"

"I will." She gave him a quick hug.

I shook his hand, "Thanks for everything."

"Good luck you guys and don't you worry about a thing I'll handle your disappearance."

Before he could get to far a sudden thought came to me, "Hey Andrew!" I said.

He turned and looked at me.

"Yeah?"

"You can keep the truck."

"You sure?"

"Yeah, I have no use of it now."

He got a big smile on his face, "Thanks!" He waved at us then trotted off to the boat.

Even though we were several feet from the boat I could still hear the conversation that took place.

"Let's go back to home turf Sea Bison." Andrew said.

"What about your friends?" Sea Bison said looking our way.

"What friends?" Andrew asked, "I came here alone, don't you remember?"

Sea Bison looked over the beach before answering, "Yeah, that's right. Silly me. Let's go."

He started the boat and they were on their way back across the lake water in minutes. Andrew waved one last time before they got too far away.

Definitely no turning back now... I sighed, "So where to now Fauna?"

"North."

"Hahaha, very funny. I meant which way? Where do we head for?"

She looked around a moment then, pointing, said, "That way." she then started walking 'that way'.

"Ugh." Never a straight answer with her was there? "Come on Nixie, we might as well follow."

Chapter 19
Grilled Rabbit?

We walked for what seemed like hours and hours. My legs and feet were starting to burn and ache.

"How much further are we going Fauna? It'll be dark soon." It was like four-thirty.

"There's some woods up here where we can make camp. Not too far now."

"Make camp? We have no shelter. No tent, no nothing. All I have is the stuff in my backpack and none of it is camping gear. I don't even have a first-aid kit."

"We'll make do for now. Later we can buy a cheap tent or something. Ah, here we go." She stepped off the road we had been following for miles now and walked through some bushes. Nixie and I followed.

"Fauna? How're we gonna get food and water?" I complained. Walking for half a day had left me starving and even though I had had water in my backpack, it was now long gone.

"Stop complaining. I can find food and I'm sure Nixie here can find us some water."

We walked into the wooded area for a little ways before coming upon a good spot to set up camp. It was a nice little spot, soft dirt, some bushes for cover, and even some logs to make a fire.

"Ya know. Maybe next time we can find a state park we can camp in instead of illegally camping the middle of nowhere."

"It's not illegal if they don't catch us." Fauna smiled mischievously as she put some wood into a pile.

After making a decent fire woodpile she tossed me some matches, "Start us up a fire while I go find us some game. I'll be back within an hour." And with that she flew off. I mean literally *flew* off; she had turned into a falcon of some sorts and flown away into the evening air.

I starred at the spot she had left for a moment. Still getting used to it... I shook my head, clearing it, then tried working with the matches she'd left me.

It was tough because my fingers were near frozen, the matches were so tiny, and there always seemed to be a slight breeze that was bent on diminishing the matches fire before I could light the actual wood.

Getting frustrated with the matches I finally asked Nixie for help. "Nixie, do you mind helping me keep the wind off the match?" I asked.

"Sure." She came over and blocked the breeze with her body and I finally managed to get the wood to catch fire.

"Thanks."

She sat down next to the newly born fire but didn't say anything. I had concluded earlier that she was a woman of little words for she had hardly said a thing all day.

I put my hands in front of the fire; it was

beginning to get colder with the darkening of the sky.

"Penny for your thoughts," Nixie said as moments had passed by in silence.

She was asking me? I really hadn't been thinking of anything in particular, just the fact that I was extremely hungry. But I gave her a simple answer.

"It would cost you more than a penny for my thoughts... For I think of so many things at once they all just jumble into one thought process... It's confusing, I know, I still don't understand how my mind works."

She looked into the fire, which was now burning strongly. "What were you thinking about then?" she asked.

I smiled, "Food." She smiled into the fire, amused.

"Penny for your thoughts," I said after a moment.

She looked up at me, "I was just thinking about what you were thinking of."

"What? Food?"

She nodded.

"Fauna should be back soon. I hope; I don't like being out here in the middle of nowhere. I've just never done it before. Makes me uncomfortable, ya know?"

"No."

"What?" I asked confused.

"No, I don't know. I've always lived where it's quite, not a lot of activity. I used to travel a lot too. Especially after that day..."

"What day?" I asked when she didn't continue.

"The day that my mo-" she stopped, something caught her interest. She was staring at a spot in the bushes behind me.

"What is it?" I asked. "I think our dinners here...," she said pointing.

She was right. There behind me, coming out of the bushes, was Blanket with two plump rabbits in her mouth. I kind of shuddered inwardly; I've never had rabbit before.

"Oh yea! Rabbit.... my favorite..." I said sarcastically as she changed back, "Why couldn't you have just gone to McDonald's and killed us a chicken sandwich, huh?"

"If you want to stay out of the eyes of the authorities you stay *away* from the public eye," was all she said before she sat down and produced a knife from her pocket.

She started to bring the knife up to the poor bunny. I turned away very quickly and said, "Uh, I think I'm gonna go find us some water."

I grabbed our bottles and headed off into the forest. I didn't know where to find any water but I knew I'd hurl if I stayed. It was pretty dark now so I took my watch and turned on its flashlight.

I walked a ways and then stopped, I had just realized that this was the first time I'd been completely alone in a long while. In that forest, it made me feel like I was the only person on earth. But that wasn't true.

Something rustled behind me so I pointed my

watch towards the sound. Nothing was there. I turned around, my heart jumped, there she was, her blonde hair like a beacon in the darkness.

"What are you doing? You scared me." I whispered.

"Scared you? I've been following you this whole time," she whispered back.

"Really? I didn't notice."

"Yes. I don't know why I'm following you though; the nearest water source is not the way you're going. And why are we whispering?" she added.

"I dunno. How do you know where water is?"

"Just do." She shrugged and walked off. I followed walking right next to her so we could both see where we were going.

The nearest water source turned out to be a small pond. Nixie and I filled our filtering bottles to the brim, drank our fill, and then filled them again. I was in the lead on the way back, having memorized the way.

"What gave you the sudden urge to fetch water, Kieth?" Nixie asked as we walked.

"One. We needed it. Two. I was pretty sure I was about to throw up."

"So you've never had rabbit before?"

I nodded, "I'm really not a 'game eater'."

"You should be thankful we have any food at all. I remember some winter nights going without meat because all the game was hibernating and the traps had come up empty."

"Man, y'all had it rough back then. Nowadays I can just yell at the House to make me my drink and food. You guys had to actually *hunt* it."

"Yes, but it was not so hard, not when you know how to hunt." I slowed my pace as I saw the faint glow of the firelight. Nixie noticed this.

"Would you like me to see if she is done with the skinning so you don't throw up on the food?" she asked with a hint of a smile.

"That would be great."

She left me but soon came back to tell me it was okay.

Fauna laughed at me as I came up to the fire where the rabbits where cooking.

"Nixie here tells me you're squeamish."

"So? What if I am?" I replied.

"Get used to eating rabbit since that's the easiest thing to catch."

I set the waters down next to our bags, "It's easier to catch a 'fast food restaurant'." I mumbled under my breath.

"Foods almost done." Fauna said as she sprinkled some leafy stuff onto the rabbits.

"You have seasoning?" I asked surprised.

"I've lived in the wilderness long enough to know the good herbs from the bad herbs Kieth."

A few minutes later the food was done and I was being handed some meat on a stick. I was reluctant to eat it at first but Fauna insisted it tasted like chicken so I took a bite.

"Well?" Fauna asked, "Doesn't it taste just like

chicken?"

"Maybe," I said taking another bite so as to satisfy my hunger. Okay, so it was good... but I wasn't about to admit it.

Once we all had our fill Fauna stored the leftovers for tomorrow.

"I think we should all hit the sack. Did anyone bring blankets?" Fauna asked, "Cause I didn't."

Nixie and I both shook our heads.

"Well, that's another thing on our list. For now we'll just have to use our coats for warmth. It's supposed to get real cold tonight, so said the weatherman this morning."

"If it's all right by you both," Nixie began, "I'd rather just stay up. I don't think I could sleep even if I wanted to. I might just walk around a bit, probably go to the pond."

"Yeah, that's fine with us," Fauna said, "As long as you're here in the morning I'm good."

Nixie nodded her appreciation then got up.

"Be careful," was all I could say as she left us to our makeshift beds.

"Hey Fauna," I said as she was putting a log on the fire sometime later, "I have a question for you."

"Yeah?"

"Why did you lie to Andrew about my power?" I still felt weird calling my dreams a 'power' but I guess that's what it was no use calling it something else...

She thought for a second, "I didn't tell him because I didn't want him to know."

I rolled my eyes, "Obviously, but *why* didn't you want him to know."

"Some things are better left unknown, for the time being at least." She stoked the fire one last time before coming over and lying in a spot next to me.

"Is that the reason you didn't tell Nixie?" she asked.

"Yes," I said, "I figured since you didn't tell him I wouldn't tell her. At least, not in front of him... Is there any reason I shouldn't tell her? I mean, I think we can trust her and all."

"Of course we can trust her. You can tell her sometime tomorrow. But for now let's leave the subject and go to bed. We'll have an early start in the morning."

That was the end of our conversation, for as soon as Fauna had stopped talking she was cuddling my feet as the familiar fluffy white dog and was asleep almost instantly.

At least my feet would be warm...

~ "You're lucky that bite didn't kill you." Mr. Newark was saying, "You should be dead! She bit you with a Black Mamba! One of the most deadly snakes known to man-" Mr. Newark stopped short interrupted by another man.

"I'm aware what kind of snake bit me Nexryt. Thank you for reminding me."

Mr. Newark and Dr. Forjd were walking through a wet lab.

"I'm just glad the authorities were able to gain control back on House before we drowned," he continued.

"Yes that is very fortunate." Mr. Newark agreed but something still seemed to bother him. He walked in front of Dr. Forjd and stopped.

"The *doctors* at the hospital said you should have died Ross. So why didn't you? There must be a reason."

"Have you ever wondered who the first human Bionan test subject was?"

Mr. Newark's eyes got big, "You wouldn't have?"

"Yes and I've never regretted it. That snakebite may have been the most deadly but the Bionans destroyed the poison before it could affect me. The process just left me weak; that is why I was in the hospital for those few days. But now my body has recovered and it's time to get down to business... Where did my nephew go?" ~

I woke suddenly and jumped upright, "He's alive!" I yelled.

Fauna and Nixie both looked at me from where they were sitting by the fire. They were both warming their breakfast of rabbit; I saw a second stick in Fauna's hand, which I assumed to be mine.

I fell back down on my side holding my head in my hands.

~ "We have a location on your Ford truck. It was last seen yesterday in Glen Rose." ~

I opened my eyes; Fauna and Nixie were by my side. "He's looking for us," I told them.

"Define 'he' Kieth." Fauna said. I looked her in the eyes, "Dr. Forjd."

"Your uncle?" Nixie asked.

"Yes, and he's alive. Th-the snakebite didn't kill him. He used himself as a test subject for Bionans, and these Bionans destroyed the venom. But it left him weak and-" I groaned as my head exploded again.

~ "Glen Rose, what are we waiting for? Let's go." ~

"Kieth?" Fauna said as she shook me.

"I'm fine, I'm fine."

"What's going on here?" Nixie asked.

I'd like to know that too...

"Yes, what were you saying? Dr. Forjds alive? I got that. But what's this about 'Bionans?'"

I had to take some calming breaths before I could answer, "Bionans are the new doctors. It's still relatively new. The only person I know with them is back at that laboratory plotting his revenge. He's coming after us. He already knows the truck is in Glen Rose... Why did I let Andrew have it?" I cursed myself. "He's in big trouble now."

"I still don't know what's going on." Nixie said,

"Do you mean to say you know what's happening with your uncle right now?"

"Uh, yeah... You could say that... I meant to tell you about it later but I guess now's better than never." I went on to explain a bit more to her, "You see, Fauna here says my 'Powerful Name' is Nevio and apparently I can see the future-"

Her eyes widened, she looked at Fauna. "You do not mean to say that he is..."

Fauna nodded. "That's not possible," Nixie said astounded.

"Uh, am I missing something here?" I said confused.

"It's nothing Kieth." Fauna said.

"It defiantly is something and I think I ought to be told what it is!"

"You don't need to know right-"

"I think I very well should know! Especially if it's concerning me-"

"Hey!" Nixie interrupted, "Now's not the time! If what Kieth has told us is true we should be on our way."

"Your right! Pack up!" Fauna agreed.

I let the anger inside me go. I wanted to get the answers to my question but it would just have to wait.

I gathered my things quickly, ate my semi warm rabbit for breakfast, and then once the others were ready we trudged off.

"Where to now?" I asked Fauna after a bit of walking.

"We're going to Kingston. It's the closest city from here. But from there we'll catch a Soar and take it to Ardmore."

"No way! Not a Soar!" I said, angry again.

"What's a 'Soar'?" Nixie asked.

"Uh, it's like a train... But it's really fast." Fauna explained but she forgot one crucial detail.

"Yeah, and it can fly..." I added, "Don't you know how I am with planes! And they're slower than the Soars."

The Soars were only used between cities while planes were used for long distance traveling. They could also carry more people meaning it was useful for workers who lived a city or two away from their work.

"What's a pla-, you know, never mind, if it's important I'll find out," Nixie said. "Come on Kieth, we gotta take a Soar. It's the fastest way to travel."

"I thought you wanted to stay away from the public." I really didn't want to get on a Soar, two plane rides was enough flying for one year.

"Not now that he's onto us! We have to get to Akira as fast as we possibly can."

I thought for a moment then said, "You're gonna make me do it no matter what I say aren't you?"

"Yep." She ran ahead of us so I couldn't say anything back to her. She also left me in an awkward silence with Nixie.

After a moment I said, "A plane flies too. They're just slower."

"Hmmmm. I've always wondered what the birds

saw when they fly so high in the sky. It must be an experience."

"Ha, yeah sure. Everything looks like ants from up there. And every moment you could fall to your death you're so high up. One malfunction of one of the systems and 'pew' down like a missile."

I knew I shouldn't be telling her all the down sides of air travel... but hey, I was nervous. I hated heights.

She looked at me, troubled.

"Sorry, it's just, I don't like heights all that much."

"Don't listen to him Nixie," Fauna had slowed down and was now with us again.

"He's just scared, that's all," she joked.

And sadly, she was right.

Chapter 20
Soar'n

"Okay," Fauna said after a while, "here's the deal. Before we get into the city I'm going to change into a dog so I only have to pay for two tickets. I'm not going to turn into Blanket though, it's too recognizable."

"You can do that?" I asked.

"Of course! I can change into any breed of any animal. I just prefer Blanket for, sentimental reasons."

"But won't it look odd? I mean a couple of kids running around the soar station with their dog?" I asked.

"Nah, it's the month of Thanksgiving. Kids will be traveling to see their grandparents and visa versa. You'll fit right in. Just say I'm your Grandmas dog you were taking care of and now you have to return me." She smiled big.

She had a plan for everything didn't she?

Just before we got into Kingston we went down a side road so Fauna could change into her dog.

"I hope you have a leash," I said.

"You won't need a leash," she said giving her bag to Nixie then she turned into a small Yorkie dog.

Before heading into the heart of town I made sure mine and Nixie's faces were well covered. I let her wear my hoodie and I wore my hat. Once I was sure we wouldn't be recognized Fauna led us to the Soar station.

Once there, Fauna allowed me to pick her up, tail waggling, and put her in my backpack.

I paid for our tickets with the money Fauna had given me earlier and then we waited for the next Soar to be ready.

"Soar to Ardmore ready to board," the intercom said just minutes later. "That's us," I told Nixie reluctantly, I still would rather walk.

We got up and boarded the Soar that said Ardmore. There were many other people that got on the Soar after us.

We quickly found two free seats; I grabbed Fauna out of my backpack and set her on my lap.

Some ladies voice told us to buckle up.

I helped Nixie with the belt then did my own. Just in time too for the engines roared to life and we began to rise off the platform.

If I had to fly, I would prefer a plane to a Soar any day for one reason and one reason only. In a Soar every seat was a window seat. The whole thing was made of fortified glass, the floor, the ceiling, everything. Apparently the creator had wanted a 'scenic view' while flying and the design just stuck.

Nixie looked around excitedly as we cleared the station and headed away from the city. I gripped Fauna harder than I probably should have but if she noticed she didn't complain... yet.

"How amazing!" Nixie said looking at the tiny houses below us, "It's like a whole new world up here!"

I had a snappy comeback but I wouldn't allow

myself to speak because if I did I'd probably yell at the captain to land this over-sized glass box now.

"The ground looks like some kind of patch work quilt!" Nixie marveled still looking all around. Meanwhile I was intensely watching the back of some persons head.

Something wet touched my hand, it was Fauna licking my hand.

"Sorry," I whispered loosening my grip.

In no time at all we arrived in Ardmore. I had to sit down for a few minutes before we headed for the edge of town. Fauna (still a Yorkie) lead the way.

Nixie was still amazed by the flight. "I've never seen flying birds that close before!" She was saying as we walked off the road and into some more woods.

I was glad to see her happy.

"Well, I'm glad *someone* enjoyed the ride." Fauna had just changed back to herself. "Unlike Mr. Scaredy Cat here! He was squeezing me so tight I thought he was going to choke me!"

I knew that would come up, "I said I was sorry... besides, I can't help it."

"Why are you afraid of flying, Kieth?" Nixie asked.

I shrugged, "I dunno. Just am and always have been. Everyone's afraid of something. My fear just happens to be heights."

We walked on a bit.

"You know? Why are we walking? We should

just rent a car or something... Especially since we're so close to Texas. You do know that Alvord is only about an hour from here, right? We should be as far away from there as we possibly can be."

She thought for a moment then sighed, "Your right... He could be on our tail any minute now and I need to keep you both away from him at any cost."

She turned around and headed back the way we came, "What're you doing?"

"We're going back to the city to get a car, and then we make a beeline for Colorado."

"You do know that I was kinda joking, right? Where are you gonna get the money to pay for or even rent a car?"

"I have my ways." The conversation ended there. By now I just went along with whatever she decided to do.

As we got back into Ardmore Fauna seemed to be counting something out on her fingers.

"What are you figuring?" I asked after she had done them twice.

"The cost."

"The cost of?"

"A car." she stopped figuring turned and looked at me, "I know you won't like what I'm about to say Kieth but we have to we don't have enough."

"No Fauna," I said catching on immediately, "we can't do that!"

"Do you want to get away from here or not?"

"Yes, I do but we can't possibly steal- ahh..." My vision blurred for a moment.

"Kieth?" Fauna questioned, "What is it?"

"Fine... You win." I pointed out a bright yellow bug that was parked on the edge of the street, "the keys are in it, the owner has a second car. Let's just get this over with."

I walked off towards the buggy leaving Fauna behind. She had had a look of 'what!?' on her face and I didn't want to answer questions I didn't know the answers to.

"Come on!" I said when I realized they hadn't followed.

Fauna approached the car first, she tried the door, it didn't budge, "Darn, I thought you said the keys were inside."

"Yeah but I didn't say it was unlocked."

"What good are keys if we can't get inside?"

"They're good when you have someone around who can get past the pass code lock on the door."

I swiped my hand near the door handle and a transparent keypad appeared. I put in the numbers I'd seen in my vision and it unlocked immediately. I opened the door, grabbed the keys, and held them out to Fauna.

She grabbed them and sat down in the driver's seat, "Showoff." I heard her mumble as she started the car.

I put my bag in the back then sat in the passenger's seat, Nixie sat in the middle of the back. After a few minutes I turned the radio on to break the dead silence. The radio was set to some Christian station. No one seemed to reject so I just left it alone and let the music play.

After a few songs the radio host started talking to the traffic watcher person saying, "Did you hear, Star, about the Amber Alert in Texas?" I turned the radio up a hair.

"Yes, it's so scary!"

"Fifteen year old, Kieth Forjd, was kidnapped from his home two days ago by an unknown woman and is still missing today. This woman is said to be dangerous. Authorities believe that she has taken him into - get this Star - they believe she has taken him over the border into Oklahoma."

"That would be tough."

"Yes it would. Red haired green eyed Kieth Forjd," he continued, "is the son of the renowned Dr. Forjd. He is also the World Genniuss Record holder for being the smartest person on earth."

"That's impressive, Teelo," Star interrupted.

"Yes it is. He also, apparently according to my notes, has a slight British accent- go figure. Dr. Forjd, currently recovering from an injury in the hospital, is wanting his son back at all costs."

"Let's just pray he's found quickly and unharmed," Star said before going over traffic things. I turned off the radio before she could finish.

"He can't possibly be in the hospital... I saw him and Mr. Newark in the lab, talking and planning on coming after us," I said troubled.

"Well," Fauna said, "I thought you saw the future, not the present?"

"I think I've seen it all before... future, present,

and past... but how am I supposed to tell which is which?"

"I dunno," she shrugged.

"Maybe," Nixie said from the back, "maybe you have to pay attention to details. Like can you see anything that would tell you what day your dream was taking place?"

"Um..." I recalled the dream to the front of my memory and looked past the people and into the background where on the wall was a digital calendar.

"There's a calendar... It says the seventh and today's the fifth."

"So that means I've got two days to get you both to Colorado," Fauna said, "I think I can do that."

"But what about Andrew?" I said, "Shouldn't we warn him or something."

"As much as I hate to say it Kieth, we can't. We would defiantly be caught and I would never be able to forgive myself."

"Would you be able to forgive yourself if Dr. Forjd captures Andrew and takes him under his command using Andrew and his power to his disposal?"

"Yes, because I know that Andrew can handle himself and he wouldn't want us coming back for him anyway." There was no going any further; she would not listen.

"I hope your right." I didn't want Andrew having to live in the same way I had the past few months.

It wasn't long before we came upon Oklahoma

City. We made good time; passing right under the upper city faster than we had thought it would take.

"Hey," Fauna said, "Why don't you mess with the GPS, see if you can get us directions from our current location to Pikes Peak Colorado."

"Bug, you heard her Pikes Peak, CO please." The directions appeared on a screen in the middle of the dashboard.

"How'd you know it could do that?" Fauna asked.

"Most cars have a House-like system built in them. This car could probably drive itself if you wanted it to."

She glared at me, "and you didn't tell me that earlier why?"

"Count it as payback for making me ride in a Soar."

"Well what are you waiting for? Change it to auto drive."

I savored my revenge for a moment longer before saying, "Bug, please auto drive to location on the GPS."

A green light appeared on the wheel and Fauna let go, not needing to drive anymore. "Thank you," she said.

The route the car had chosen took us right up through Dodge City, Kansas. After almost ten plus hours of driving we finally stopped in Pueblo, Colorado, one because we were tired of driving and two so we could find a place to sleep for the night.

It would be only an hour or so drive tomorrow morning.

My ears had begun popping as soon as we crossed the Colorado border; it reminded me of being on a plane... I did not like that feeling.

I also did not like the feeling I had had since Oklahoma City that something wasn't right. Maybe the feeling came from the 'stealing the car' thing or maybe it was an after effect of riding in a see through flying machine. I don't know, I just didn't like it.

"Hey we need to stop by a supermarket," Fauna was saying as we pulled into the main part of town, "We need food and stuff."

"Isn't that a bad idea seeing as I'm on the Amber Alert in all of North America?"

We had heard more on the radio about my apparent kidnapping since Oklahoma.

"Just put on your hoodie."

"What do we even need anyway? Especially now that we have the car."

"Well..." she hesitated, as she pulled into the supermarkets parking lot.

"What now?" I sighed.

"We need to ditch the car." I started to protest but she interrupted me, "The owner of this car has by now figured out its gone and is probably on our trail right now. We don't need that kind of attention. What we need to do is disappear back into the woods. And don't worry it's only a day's journey to Pikes Peak from here."

She parked the car and we all got out. I put on my hoodie; it was at times like these I didn't like my hair.

"I'm sure Nixie agrees with me, right Nixie?" Fauna said as we walked towards the large double story building.

Nixie thought for a moment before giving an answer, "Seeing as how I'm still new to everything I'm not sure I can give a good answer but if it is as Fauna says and they are 'on our trail' then we should do whatever it takes to get them off it."

"Fine, majority wins but don't come crying to me when you end up carrying all our stuff tomorrow," I joked.

The supermarket wasn't as full as it could have been but thankfully there were enough people to blend in with.

The first place we went was to the 'sporting goods' section. There Fauna bought two cheap pocket tents; they were of decent size. She also asked the man at the counter where the nearest state park was.

"Pueblo State Park just west of here," he said giving us a brochure.

"Thank you."

After that we then got some food, flashlights, and other cheap camping stuff.

We brought our bags out to the car and to my surprise Fauna put the groceries in and started the car.

"What?" she said when I gave her a funny look.

"I didn't say we had to ditch it tonight did I?"

I hopped in after her; grateful she wasn't about to make us walk just yet.

Chapter 21
Wishes

The GPS led us straight to the state park where we paid a night's fee. We set up camp at the site we were given.

I did the tents while Nixie helped Fauna with the fire.

"I hope we're not having rabbit for dinner again?" I said once the tents were up.

I went over and sat by the fire.

"No actually, I thought we'd have this popcorn we bought." She went to go dig through the grocery bags.

"Sounds good."

It wasn't long before I heard the sound of the popcorn popping in its pan. After it was done we each got our own share to eat.

"Hey," Fauna said, "Y'all wanna go down to the restrooms and wash up before bed?" Nixie and I agreed, and we then quickly got our stuff together to go wash off.

I was the first back from the showers. It felt weird walking back to the tent in my pajamas. Sure, it was dark and I had a coat on but still it just wasn't normal. Luckily there was hardly anyone at any of the tent sites; all the smart people were probably in an RV area in a nice warmly heated bed or something.

I unzipped my tent and got in. I was thankful for the insulation that kept the warm air trapped in the tent because my wet hair had almost frozen on the short walk from the restroom to the tent.

I was exhausted from the day's events so I crawled into my sleeping bag and closed my eyes. I didn't fall asleep but it felt good just to lie there and do nothing.

I listened to the sound of the wind blowing through the trees and the crickets playing their songs.

Eventually I heard the footsteps of Fauna and Nixie. They had their own tent, as it would have looked odd for Nixie and I if Fauna had decided to be an animal versus her human self.

They didn't bother me as they went into their tent; they probably thought I was sleeping.

Hours later, in the middle of the night, I heard the rustling of fabric. Something, or someone, was moving over in the girls' tent. Light footsteps walked away from the tent; I could tell it was Nixie.

I silently got out of my sleeping bag, put my shoes and coat on, and slipped outside.

She had walked down one of the paths that was nearest our tents. I followed her down this path that brought us all the way to the lake. Here she stopped and sat by the edge. I stopped too, just on the edge of the path, I didn't want to disturb her just yet.

A few minutes passed and still she sat there not doing a thing. So I decided I'd leave her alone and go but as I turned around to do so Nixie said, "I know your there."

I came from my hiding spot and sat down next to

her, "How'd you know?"

She merely replied, "There is water in basically everything, or everyone, and I can sense the water that is in it."

"Hmm." The human body *is* mostly made of water. "So why are you out here?" I asked.

"I can't sleep." She paused for a moment then continued, "Why are you out here?"

"I heard you get up and followed you, besides." I shrugged. "I couldn't sleep either."

We sat there for the longest time. I looked over the lake, occasionally I would see a fish jump out of the water; catching a nighttime bug probably. Thankfully my jacket was warm because the wind coming off the water was numbing.

"Look!" Nixie said all of a sudden pointing towards the cloudless sky, "it's a falling star! Make a wish."

Despite the fact that I knew falling stars were only burning rocks from outer space, I closed my eyes and made a wish anyway.

"What did you wish for?" I asked after a moment.

She sighed, "You would probably think it silly."

"Well I won't know till you tell me."

"I wished for my life back..." She paused. "Or at least to understand the reason behind why everything has happened the way it's happened. And every time I look at you," she continued, "I'm reminded of what I lost. My friends are gone, gone forever. I just wish I knew what happened to them."

I could tell she was almost crying.

"Nixie," I whispered, "I wasn't entirely honest with you the other night..."

"What do you mean?" She sniffed.

"I have an idea of what happened to your friends..." And so I told her what I knew from the dream I had had.

"...So," I finished, "I'm assuming they were made prisoners... And that's all I know, and I'm sorry I didn't tell you sooner."

She didn't respond right away but I could see her shoulders begin to shake.

"My- friends... prisoners... gone." Back to square one.

"Hey." I put a reassuring hand on her. "Your friends may be gone but they live on in your memory and even in your new friends. But they will never die as long as you keep them in your heart."

She looked at me, a hopeful gleam in her eye, "Really?"

"Yeah, I'm sure of it."

She gave me a small smile then looked up towards the stars. After a moment she said, "You asked me, now it's my turn. What did you wish?"

"Me..." I hesitated, "Well, I wished that, for just *one* night, that I wouldn't have any dreams. None at all."

"Why would you not want to have any dreams?" she asked, "Dreams are where you can do anything. It's where you get to see your imagination run wild."

"Well, I see things differently. In my dreams I see things that are going to happen and I'm forced to have these dreams... And it's not like I know how to control them."

I was just ranting now, "You know, I don't see how me being a Powerful is really all that great. I mean how is being able to see the future a power when I can't even control when and what I see?"

She thought for a long moment then said, "I don't know how to tell you how being a Powerful is great, seeing as we are wanted for lab rats, but I do know it's a gift.

"My mother once told me that each of us gets a different gift and we have to learn how to use our gift to help others. And you have one of the best gifts Kieth, you could help a lot of people- just believe in yourself."

I thought about what she said and she was right. I had to believe that I could control whatever was controlling me, if that was even the case.

"Nixie, about my 'gift'... I'm sorry I didn't tell you the truth. I should have told you before."

"It's okay," was all she said, "I may have done the same thing in your situation."

"Yeah, I guess its not every day that you find out that your father is actually your uncle and your dog is your sister..."

She gave a little laugh, "I bet that was a surprise."

"Hmmm... yeah, it was and I'm still just getting over it." She smiled at me but quickly turned her attention to the water.

I sat in silence as she moved some water around the air, she didn't seem to be doing anything with it other than move it here and there but it was cool to watch it hovering there in the air.

"So tell me," I said after a while of watching her move the water around. "What is it that you and Fauna were keeping from me this morning?"

The water she had had in the air dropped to the ground as if she lost concentration or something.

"I should not be the one to tell you."

"And why not?"

"Because it is not my place to do so, not yet anyway and defiantly not now."

"Fine." I yawned. "I guess I'll figure it out someday."

"Someday but not today."

I yawned again.

"Are you not tired?" Nixie asked. "Today was a long day."

"I'm terribly tired."

"Then why not go to sleep?" she asked.

I wrapped my arms around my legs before answering, "Because I'm scared."

"Scared of what?"

"My dreams," I said simply, "They just feel more like horrible nightmares than good dreams and I have them most every night. It's nerve racking."

"I'm sorry."

"You don't have to be, it's not your fault."

She went to moving around some water again.

"Aren't you cold?" I asked after noticing she was wearing a short-sleeved shirt.

"No not really."

"Honestly? Because I'm a Popsicle and I have a jacket on."

She shrugged, "It has something to do with my Power. I'd explain but it's complicated."

"Hmmmm, well you'll have to explain it to me one day." I then decided to ask her a question that had been in the back of my mind for a while, "Nixie, what does the mark on your arm mean?"

The water fell to the ground again as she turned her left arm over to show me. "You mean this?"

"Ya, Fauna has one like it but I just haven't asked about it yet."

"It's called 'The Mark of a Powerful'. We are given our mark when we have some amount of control over our given power."

"What do the strange symbols mean?" I asked.

"It is my Powerful name. And the symbols are just the letters we use to write with, they are pronounced the same way as we speak now but just written differently."

"Wow, do you think you could teach me? It wouldn't take long."

"Of course, I can show you the letters tomorrow when there is more light."

"Awesome, so what does the other mark represent?"

"This?" she said indicating the 's' shaped lines, "it represents water coming out of a river."

"Cool."

"Yes, each mark is different to each Powerful and a different color is given to each depending on their status. For example, I am a princess I would have a different color than one of my people. There are six different colors, so therefore six ranks. But the ranks are earned and not just given, except in special cases..."

"Sounds complicated."

"Not really."

After a little while of silence I got up, deciding that I should at least try and get some sleep before we had to walk all day tomorrow.

"Coming with me?" I asked.

"No."

"Okay, now it's my turn to ask, how can you not be tired? As far as I know you haven't slept at all since Glen Rose. Am I right?"

"Yes, your right I have not slept since waking in Glen Rose. But I'm not tired and whenever I do try to sleep I can't."

She didn't seem to want to talk anymore so I said, "See you in the morning then?"

"I'll be there."

"Good night Nixie." I walked off back towards camp but before I got too far I heard her speak towards the water.

"Good night Nevio."

~ There he was, tied to a chair with a gag in his mouth. He was staring intensely at the two men who were sitting across from him.

"So now what do we do?" Mr. Newark asked. "We can't have him say anything since we'll end up hitting each other with our shoes or something!"

"We are exactly where we need to be Nexryt." Dr. Forjd said, "Now that we know where he is he cannot escape even if he wants to."

Dr. Forjd fiddled with his watch.

"Can we put a blindfold on him? His stare is starting to scare me."

"Whatever's needed," he said as he popped up an image on his watch. It was of a boy in a hoodie standing with two girls in the checkout line of a supermarket. On his watch, the date read, 11-5-31. ~

I woke feeling more confused than ever before.

"Fauna, I'm so confused," I told her after I had woken her up and explained what I had seen, "I don't know what's real. What do I believe?"

"I dunno Kieth. I'm just as confused as you are," she confessed.

"Well I do know something." I said.

"What's that?"

"We *have* to rescue Andrew."

Her face saddened at my words. "Kieth, we can't. We just can't risk it. Anyways, he's probably all the way in Texas."

"No. He's here, I'm sure of it."

"Who's here?" Nixie asked, she had just come from the trail I'd followed her down late last night.

"Dr. Forjd, he's here in Pueblo."

"How do you know?" Fauna asked.

"I dunno," I shook my head, "I just have a feeling he's here."

"What did I miss now?" Nixie said and I explained my dream over again to her.

"Sounds like Andrew needs our help," she said.

"That's what I've been saying! We have to go and help him."

"No." Fauna interrupted, "I can't let you do that! I have to get you to Akira."

"Why is it so important to get me to Akira? Hmmm? Why? What good will it do; he'll find me either way. I don't know how but he will."

"But that's why I have to take you to him Kieth! He can help get Dr. Forjd off our tail!"

"How? How will he get him off our trail?"

She gave me a hesitant answer, "I'll know when we get there..."

The image of Andrew gagged and tied to a chair flashed through my head again, "No," I said, "you won't know, because I'm not going."

"Kieth, c'mon we gotta-"

"No Fauna! You don't understand. Andrew's in trouble and I have to go help him. He helped me, now I have to help him back. If you can't get that then fine, go to Akira; but as for me, I'm going to find Andrew."

Without a second thought I grabbed my things and started off in the direction I knew I should go but I stopped and asked, "Nixie? Are you with me?"

I continued when she didn't answer, "He helped

all of us you know."

She thought for a moment then grabbed her own things and joined me saying, "I'm with you. I don't want another person to have to become a prisoner because of me."

"Fauna?" I asked one last time, "Are you coming?"

After a moment she sighed, I knew she had given in, "I'm gonna skin Andrews hide for this."

I smiled, happy she was coming with us. "I guess we can get the rest of our stuff then."

We packed up real quick and cleaned up the campsite before hopping in the yellow bug.

"I thought we were gonna ditch it?" I asked when we left the campsite a few minutes later, "not that I'm complaining or anything."

"I decided we'd get to our destination quicker if we drive... speaking of, where am I supposed to be going?"

"Hold on, let me think for a moment."

I had no real idea where he was; all I knew at the moment was that he was in Pueblo the same as us but where I could not guess.

I recalled my dream and looked over the details of the room hoping to find some answers but it was useless seeing as the room had no windows or anything marking it as anything but blank walls.

"Aah, this is hopeless," I said after minutes of looking but finding nothing. "Let's just ride around town; maybe we'll find something that way."

And that's just what we did until about twelve in the afternoon. By that time I had memorized pretty much the whole town and still nothing seemed to scream out at me.

We stopped at some fast food chain that was across from the supermarket we had gone to last night.

"So what exactly are we looking for? Like what type of building?" Fauna asked as we were eating our lunch.

"Well, about all I know is that there were no windows and also an elevator? So I guess it could be some kind of basement or something? Also it looked like a really big room."

"That's a start I guess. Basement with an elevator, that means that either its far underground or the person it belongs to is just plain lazy."

After we were done eating we kinda just sat there collecting our thoughts. One of the workers came by, asked if we were done, and offered to take our trash. We said that we were done and she collected our trash but before she could leave Fauna asked,

"Miss? Do you know of any large basements around here? Large enough to have to have an elevator?"

The lady thought for a moment before answering, "The only one I really know of is at the supermarket across the street. See I used to work there and the basement is where we kept the merchandise and it did have an elevator access."

"Thank you," Fauna said as she left, "Do you

think it could be it Kieth?"

"I don't know. It could be but if it was how do we get down there? It would be staff only right?"

"We'll just have to see. C'mon," she said getting up, "It's time we left."

"We're never gonna find the entrance," I said after about twenty minutes of wandering around the multilevel supermarket, "We should have asked that girl."

"If we just stay on ground level we're sure to find it," Fauna said, though she didn't seem too sure either.

We walked into multiple elevators checking them for any sign that it might take us below ground level. Even after going through every elevator we could find, we couldn't find anything that would take us to a basement.

We were taking a short cut through the liquid paint aisle when something caught my eye. It was a door, an employee door, someone had just gone through it and in that brief moment I caught a glimpse of the shining metal doors of an elevator.

"Guys wait," I said as I pointed towards the doors, "I'm pretty sure we won't find what we're looking for out here. The only logical place they'd have access to the lower levels is from the employees' side of the building. They wouldn't have all of the elevators capable of going below if only the employees use it... in there is what we need, I'm sure of it."

Fauna examined the door with careful eyes; her

dull brown hair was pulled up in a high ponytail. "We've got to get an ID card or else that door won't open for us, so the elevator probably won't either."

"What do we do then?" Nixie asked.

"We have to get an ID card from one of the workers." I said, simply stating the obvious. "But how?"

Nixie and I both looked at Fauna.

She saw our gaze and said, "Do you expect me to come up with a plan every time?" We said nothing. She sighed. "Fine. Here's what we'll do..."

After watching the doors for about thirty minutes we figured that at least two employees come out or head back in every five minutes, either for the start or the end of their shift. So we would only have five minutes to work with but our plan wouldn't take much time.

I glanced at my watch. 2:00. Five more minutes there should be a shift that will go into the doors.

I was standing around the corner a few aisles away from the doors, hidden and out of sight. I glanced at my watch again. 2:02. Why couldn't time move faster?

It was at 2:04 that I heard a small group of people walking down the back aisle, finally my cue to act.

I had acquired a shopping cart before the girls left me so now I pushed that shopping cart, now filled with paint cans, into the back isle, just as the small group was walking by. Just as planned they walked into it sending the cart and its contents rolling across the floor. Two of the paint cans (intentionally tampered with) burst open and stained the polished white floors green and red. Some of the paint also ended up on one of the three employees.

2:05. Five minutes.

"Oh my gosh!" I stammered, "I'm so so sorry!" I helped the paint splattered girl up and then I tried to wipe off the paint but unbeknownst to her I grabbed her ID card and slipped it into my pocket.

As this event was taking place Fauna and Nixie came from behind (with yet another shopping cart) and 'accidentally' ran into the two employees that had not fallen.

"Oh no!" Fauna exclaimed when they were both on the ground moments later, "I didn't see you there! Are you both okay?"

2:06. We needed to hurry things up. I started frantically grabbing paint cans as Fauna and Nixie helped up their two victims.

We all apologized multiple times. They said it was nothing, just an accident, so they let us on our way as they started to clean up the mess we had made.

As we walked away the one girl I had helped up said something to her friends,

"Did anyone else get the feeling that the boy looks strikingly familiar? Like someone off of TV?"

"You think everyone looks like someone off of TV, Miranda. It was just a coincidence."

"No I'm serious," she said, "He looks like that

Forjd kid... What was his name?"

"That's ridiculous! What would Kieth Forjd be doing in Colorado?"

That was the last I could make out of their conversation as we approached the doors.

2:07. Time to go through the doors. We all got the ID cards we had pick-pocketed and swiped them past the handle. The doors opened. We were in.

We quickly made a dash for the elevator. I got there first and pressed the button, a few seconds later the doors open and we rushed inside. No one was in there. I pressed the button for the basement and down it went.

"Okay," Fauna panted, "We're in. Now what?"

"You mean you don't have any more plans?" I asked her.

She shook her head. "And even if I did I wouldn't know the first place to look for Andrew. I'm following you now Kieth."

"But-" I paused, "but I don't even know where he is! For all I know he's in another basement down the street!"

"Then why this basement? Something more than dumb luck brought us here. Heck, if it wasn't for you Kieth we wouldn't be down here looking for him in the first place."

"It's not like I have a map Fauna!"

The elevator doors slid open.

"Well we better figure something out fast or we're dead meat."

We wandered the endless halls for a few minutes.

It was nothing like in my dreams. Yet I knew we had to be here.

"Times a wasting Kieth! Those workers are gonna clean up our mess and figure out their ID cards are missing any minute now. You gotta think, where is he."

"I don't know," I said helplessly. "You know I can't control it."

"Well you have to try! We're almost out of time."

"Don't you think I am!" I snapped back at her. I knew how much trouble we'd be in if we were caught. I knew that Andrew might not in fact be here. I knew it was all a-

"Trap." I said out loud.

"What?" Fauna said.

"It's a trap." All I could do was fall to my knees as random images flashed through my head. I wasn't able to make out what they were but they kept flashing by.

"The boy's right," said an achingly familiar voice, "You are caught like a mouse in a rat trap."

"Nexryt!" Fauna hissed at him. "You can hardly catch a mouse unless you *are* a cat. And guess who the mouse is today?"

She turned into a cat and jumped at him claws aimed at his face. Nexryt stood as calm as ever with his hands clasped behind his back.

"Fauna, no!" I yelled but it was too late Nexryt had produced a bag from behind him and caught Fauna right before she could even touch his face.

"Now who's the 'cat in the bag'?" he said

mockingly. I put my hands to my head...

So many images...

"Kieth," Nixie pulled on my arm, "get up! We have to get out of here." I couldn't get up and even if I could we were completely trapped. Two men stopped behind Mr. Newark waiting for orders.

"I've got the animal. Grab the other two and follow me," he said.

Nixie looked ready to put up a fight as the men approached her but Mr. Newark stopped her saying, "I wouldn't fight if I were you my dear. Remember who's got the cat."

She looked defeated as she put her hands in the air. The one man took her hands and tied them behind her back; he also stabbed her in the arm with a small needle like thing.

"Kieth," she sounded panicky. "Kieth I can't see!"

I felt so helpless as the other man dragged me to my feet and stabbed me too and almost instantly my vision went completely dark. Shadow stabbers! They used shadow stabbers on us. They were usually only in possession of police officers, able to blind someone in a matter of seconds without causing any permanent harm. Why did these guys have them?

"Calm down Nixie." I could hear her breathing hard. "It's only temporary."

The complete darkness didn't help any with my visions, because now that's all I saw. Random flashes, bits and pieces of information that didn't make any sense whatsoever. And then there was the pain. The pain in my head but also the pain in my heart as it ached.

Why had I told them to come here? It was a fool thing to do! Why couldn't I just be normal?

We were walked (or in my case, dragged) through many hallways. I knew that we had already been down this one. They must be trying to confuse us maybe in case we tried to escape.

Finally we came to a stop. The man that had me sat me in a chair and tied my hands to the back.

I could hear Fauna hissing and screeching to my left, she must still be in the bag.

I heard movement to my right. I also heard muffled screaming behind me, and the screeching of a chair against the floor.

But the movement I was most fixed on was of the quiet sounds in front of me. The shuffling of feet, whispers to another. The voice of the one I had lived with all my life.

"Hello Dad..." I said in his direction, "Or should I even call you that anymore!"

"Quell the shadow stabbers," he said calmly.

Another poke in my arm, and soon my eyes watered as bright light hit them. As my eyes adjusted I saw that Nixie was sitting in a chair to my right, she was blinking fast; she had just been stabbed too. Fauna was still in the bag in Mr. Newark's hands though she had calmed down, probably so she could hear what was going on.

There he was, standing next to Mr. Newark and three other people. A woman, and two children it looked like but it was too dark where they were standing to make out their faces.

He glared at me, studying me. After a moment he turned his eyes upon Nixie and looked her over too.

"I see you have awakened from your slumber Princess," he said walking up to her, "And in such prime condition. You truly are a living relic."

"Don't touch her!" I yelled as he grabbed her chin to point her face upwards. He looked at her as if he was looking at some laboratory specimen.

"Kieth," he said as if I hadn't said anything at all, "It's high time I introduce you to someone." He held his hand out to the woman. I gasped as she came into the light. I knew her.

"Kieth this is my wife, your mother, Tess *Atia* Forjd."

Chapter 22
Either Peace or War

"No," I whispered. This was the woman that was in my photos. The one I had believed was my dead mother all my life. "It can't be! You're wrong! You're not my father! I don't even know how I can call you my uncle!"

"Be quiet," he snapped, "I'm not done with introductions." He waved over the two children; one was a girl and the other a boy. They both had summer blonde hair and deep brown eyes and their facial features resembled the other so I assumed they could only be twins. They also looked to be about my age.

"Aut Pax." He motioned at the boy. "And Aut Belluma. My children, your real siblings." Fauna hissed from within her bag.

Aut Pax, Aut Belluma, why would he give them such horrible Latin names? 'Aut pax aut bellum' meant 'either peace or war', what was he trying to say?

"You lie, Fauna is my real sibling." He gave me a laugh, "You honestly believe her over your own father?"

"Yes, because you are not my father." I closed my eyes as more images whizzed through my head.

"I do believe it's your turn to introduce us to your new friend Kieth." I ignored him and said something different instead.

"I don't understand."

"What is there to not understand? All I want is the name of this relic."

"No, not that. I don't understand why you have kept hidden from me all these secrets. Why live with me, and me alone, when you have a wife and kids? Why keep them out of your life and me in it?"

"Pax and Belluma, as you may have already guessed, are twins and they are older than you. When you were born and we found out you were a Powerful we figured the twins would get jealous of their little brother. So we went our separate ways I took you and Tess took the twins."

I pretty much knew his answer already but hearing him say it out loud confirmed it. He was lying again.

Something dropped to the floor. It was the bag that Fauna was in, but it had grown bigger; she must've changed back.

"Oh, grow up you kooky scientist!" I heard her say, "Don't you realize that Kieth won't believe your fairy tale stories anymore. You're obviously lying!" She hesitated for the slightest moment then said, "Right Kieth?"

I couldn't answer. If I did I would give away how much my head hurt at the moment. My head lolled to one side but quickly jerked back. Now I was facing the possibility of fainting but I would not allow myself to do that when my friends were counting on me.

"Oh I'm sorry," Dr. Forjd said as if he had forgotten something important but really didn't care,

"I forgot to turn off the Bionans' didn't I?"

He grabbed something from his lab coat, it looked like some old-fashioned garage door opener but with many more buttons on it. He pressed one of those buttons now and almost instantly the pain in my head went away, and the images disappeared. I felt normal again.

"What..." I asked perplexed then my eyes widened as I realized what he was talking about and what had just happened

He must've known what my expression meant for he said, "Yes Kieth. You were always my best test subject. With the Bionans I have been able to control some of what you see but unfortunately I was never able to see the real dreams you had, that is why I had you keep a journal and that way I could 'see' them too. You are truly one of a kind."

"You- you've been placing false images in my head this whole time." No one messed with my mind.

"Not the whole time only when you needed a push."

"How could you!" Fauna yelled. "You tricked him!"

"Or more accurately put, Miss Fauna, I helped him."

"How?" I asked. "How is kidnapping and tying me to a chair considered 'help?'"

"Just trust me," he said. "Things will turn to the better if you do."

"You lost my trust weeks ago! And I'm not ready

to trust you again."

He ignored me as his watch started beeping, he tapped it, and it stopped.

"Excuse me," he said, "I'm late for an appointment. Pax! Belluma!" they both straightened at the sound of their names, "Keep an eye on our friends here would you. The adults have to go talk."

He went for the door, Mr. Newark, and Tess followed.

"We'll be back within an hour." And with that they were gone leaving us all at the hands of Peace and War.

No one said a thing and the room got unnaturally quiet. Pax and Belluma were in the far corner of the room staring us down and occasionally they would whisper among one another but I could not discern anything from their conversations.

"Andrew?" I finally whispered, "Are you alright?"

I wished I could turn around to see him, but his calm muffled voice told me that he was okay.

"How about you Fauna?"

"If you count that I've suddenly become a claustrophobic then yeah, I'm just great."

She was fine.

"Nixie?"

"A little ruffled but okay." She paused before saying, "Now what?"

I sighed, "I dunno. We find a way to escape I guess."

I glanced at Pax and Belluma. They were still looking at us, I wasn't sure if they could hear us, but I didn't really care.

"Guys, I'm sorry I got y'all into this mess. It's all my fault," I confessed.

"What are you talking about?!" Fauna exclaimed. "It is defiantly not your fault. Don't start blaming yourself for things you didn't cause. Dr. Forjd tricked you. He could have tricked any of us but-"

I interrupted her, "But it had to be me. He tricked me and I believed it. I'm the one who got us all caught, and now you're all in danger because of-"

"Me," Nixie said.

"What?" Fauna and I said. I didn't know why she would be blaming herself she did absolutely nothing wrong.

"It was me that Dr. Forjd was looking for in the first place, and if I had finished my job in Alaska those many years ago none of us would be here now."

"But it's because of me that he found you!" I said.

"Hey!" Fauna interrupted in a harsh whisper, "stop blaming each other and try to make an escape plan before I die of suffocation!"

"Here's an escape plan," I said sarcastically. "How about you turn yourself into a dragon or something and fly us out of here! Cause as of right now I'm tied to a chair if you didn't know!"

She snorted, "Kieth the closest I've ever gotten to a dragon is the Komodo Dragon, and in case you didn't know, they can't fly. Anyways I can't change. I've tried but it feels like there's something blocking me from doing it and it makes my head spin." she sighed, "If someone could only un-gag Andrew we'd be home free."

Andrew gave a muffled agreement.

"I have something I can do," Nixie said hesitantly, "But it'll take a moment or two because it requires concentration."

"Do it!" Fauna sounded almost desperate, "I need fresh air; this bag really isn't very porous."

"Okay, just go along with whatever happens okay?" Fauna and I agreed. Nixie closed her eyes in concentration but before she could do whatever she had planned Pax and Belluma came over to us from where they had been.

Pax stood before me, his brown eyes looked frightened, and he said four words that I wouldn't have guessed would ever come from his lips, "We want to help."

"Excuse me?" I asked taken by surprise.

"Don't believe him!" Fauna said from her bag. "He's probably under Dr. F's control!"

"No," he said quickly, "please listen! Father is lying; we actually do have powers. We just didn't really get them naturally I guess. He's been experimenting on us all our lives, trying to make us more like you."

He stopped Belluma continued what he was saying, "He failed of course, and that is why he wants you so bad. He wants to be in control of your futuristic powers. He wants to use you to either make a horrible peace or a forced war."

She pointed at Pax, and then herself, "but we've decided we don't want that and we know if we don't help you now... well..."

Pax continued, "If we don't help you now we won't ever have a real peace. So please, trust us."

They waited for my answer. I wasn't sure of what to say. Should I really trust them?

"Don't believe a word they say Kieth! This could have all been set up by him!" Fauna said.

But Andrew cut her off with hurried muffled shouts of "Ooo oooo! Elieve em!"

I couldn't very well understand Andrews words so all I said was, "Untie us and then we'll see."

They did what I said, untying Nixie and I first, then Pax released Andrew's hands, and Belluma untied Fauna's bag.

As soon as Fauna was free she pounced onto Belluma, pinning her to the ground. "What filthy trick is this!" she said tightening her grip on Belluma.

"Fauna stop!" Andrew yelled at her as soon as he had taken the gag out of his mouth, "Their words are true!"

Fauna stayed where she was. Pax looked about ready to tackle Fauna if he had to.

"Fauna," I said quietly, "Believe Andrew. This is now our escape plan."

She let go, and the tension in the room relaxed some. However, I noticed that Fauna kept a watchful eye on both the twins.

I looked at Pax, "Lead us out of here." Belluma headed to the door. I took Nixie aside for a moment, "What were you going to do?" I asked her.

She just smiled, "I'll tell you later."

"Darn it! Pax, it's locked!" Belluma said after having tried the door.

"Stand back," he said holding his hands up towards the door. A moment later the door swung open having unlocked.

"Your 'power' I presume?" Fauna asked coldly. "Yes," he said, "I am able to 'open' anything."

She whispered something under her breath and walked out the door. "So which way is it?" she asked. "Left, right, or straight?"

Pax and Belluma looked at each other with worried expressions.

Nixie saw this exchange and said, "You don't know the way out do you?"

"No, we don't." Belluma said gravely, "This place is a maze and this is the first time we've been here. So of course-"

"We don't know the way out." Pax said completing her sentence.

"I know the way." I said, saying something before Fauna could get angry again.

"How?" Pax and Belluma said, "This is your first time here too."

I was slightly surprised that Dr. Forjd hadn't told them about my photographic ability since he had been so obviously proud about it but I set the thought aside for now.

"I memorized the way," was all I said. "Come on." I led the way taking the left hallway, my friends and the twins following behind like lost sheep.

It thankfully didn't take too long to find the elevator that we had come down upon. We all piled in as soon as it opened except Pax and Belluma. I extended my hand to them, "Come with us. You won't have to live with him anymore."

"We can't," they declined, "when you escaped he placed trackers on the both of us. He'd just find you even faster if we came with you."

"I'm sorry," I said, feeling partially responsible.

"Don't be, we had a feeling it was coming anyway."

"Kieth lets go," Fauna said. "It's been at least thirty minutes since he left we don't have that much time left."

"Wait!" Andrew said. "I need to do something if they aren't coming with us."

"Whatever it is hurry up!" Fauna said quickly holding the elevator door open with her hand.

Andrew turned to Pax and Belluma saying, "When Dr. Forjd asks you both why you are wandering the hallways you'll tell him that we escaped, and you were looking for us... but you never found us, right?"

As soon as Andrew spoke they got a faraway look in their eyes. "Yes," they said in unison.

"Thank you, now go wander the hallways until

someone finds you." They both turned at his urging and left.

Suddenly Andrew put his arm out. "Not you Fauna," he sighed. "Get back in the elevator."

Fauna, who had been ready to follow Pax and Belluma down the endless hallways, snapped out of her trance and got back in the elevator.

I had the weirdest thought as the elevator ascended to the main floor that was somewhere above us. What was Belluma's power?

I shook the thought from my head, and instead thought about the matter at hand. Escaping. The elevator doors opened as we came to a stop.

"Okay," I said, "So remember that the three employees must be frantic wondering where their ID cards are and once they see us... who knows what'll happen."

"So let's try and stick together. Got it?" Fauna said. She was in a 'gung-ho' mood.

"Well yeah, that'd be great but I was thinking more along the lines of 'distraction'."

"What have you got in mind?" Andrew said. We were at the door now.

I gave them a sly smile, "Remember the paint buckets Nixie?" She smiled back, catching on. A few moments later we strolled out the staff only door.

"Hey! You kids! Stop there!" Someone yelled at us. We ignored them of course and continued walking towards the paint aisle.

Once there, we got cornered. There was a guy, a

girl (the same one who 'recognized' me) in front, and two new guys in the back.

"You stole our ID cards!" the girl yelled as they all walked in a little closer.

"You're going to have to come with us kids," said one of the guys behind us.

Now they were close enough that they could have reached out and grabbed us if they had wanted to. But I wasn't about to give them that chance.

"Now Nixie!"

She was already prepared for as soon as I said the words paint came bursting out of their cans and into the aisle.

The three men were spattered with paint, the poor girl got splatter with paint for a second time that day.

Nixie had thankfully kept the worst of the paint fountains off of us, but we still got some on us anyway.

"Go!" Fauna shouted leading the way.

We all ran after her, Andrew shouting, "We were never here!" behind him as he ran. We found the nearest exit, making it out of the supermarket (but not without many odd stares from passer-bys).

"What now?" Nixie shouted at Fauna.

"Um, we'll take the car, so we can have a quick getaway, but we'll abandon it thirty minutes or so out of the city."

And that's exactly what we did. Fauna and Andrew in the front, Nixie and I squeezed into the back.

We made it into the evening traffic without any troubles and only when we were fifteen minutes out did my nerves calm down.

After a moment of looking out the front window I noticed Nixie staring at me. She smiled when I looked at her.

"What?" I asked suspiciously.

"Your hair looks good with streaks of yellow in it." She laughed at me as I struggled to look into the rear view mirror.

She was right I had bright yellow streaks in my hair. My hood must've fallen off at some point.

"Man," I said, "Hope it washes out fast." I pulled my hood back on hiding my stupid hair.

"Hey guys," Andrew said moments later, "I want to thank y'all for saving me. I don't know what I would have done otherwise. Dr. Forjd's a mad man."

"You're welcome," I said, "But what I want to know is how did you get caught in the first place?"

"He 'ambushed' me, took me by surprise. They learned quickly what I could do and gagged me. They brought me here looking for you Kieth."

He looked accusingly at Fauna, "Why didn't you tell me? I would've come along."

"You didn't need to know at the time," she said discreetly.

"But if I had known that Kieth was-"

Fauna suddenly pulled the car over to the side of the road and stopped making us all fall forward in our seats (I was surprised the airbags didn't deploy).

"Get out. We're stopping now."

"Obviously!" I shouted, rubbing my head that had hit the seat in front of me. We all got out except for Fauna. "Aren't you coming?" I asked.

"No, I'm gonna drive a little ways more then drop off the car. Don't worry I'll catch up." She smiled then was back on the road with the other cars, which probably didn't even notice (or care) that we had stopped and gotten out.

"Umm... So does anyone know which way we're supposed to be going?" Andrew asked.

"Pikes Peak," I said pointing it out. It was probably a good thirty-minute drive from here, so a good long walk was ahead of us.

After an hour or so of walking a bird landed on Andrews head, spooking him.

Startled, he began flailing his hands around his head trying to get the bird off. "Get off, get off, get off!" He yelled, still waving his hands at the bird that was now pecking his head.

I gave a little chuckle, "Fauna, get off Andrews head."

She gave Andrews head one last peck, jumped off, and then turned back into herself. She only shrugged at Andrew's angry glare and said with a smile, "I was only playing."

Then she got serious, "Okay, team meeting." She pointed to the ground and we all sat down.

"So what'd you do with the car?" I asked when she didn't say anything.

She gave me a sly smile. "Let's just say I drove it off a cliff."

"Are you serious!"

She nodded, "Now they won't be able to follow us."

She put her hands up before I could ask another question, "I didn't call this team meeting to talk about the car; it's history. I wanted to tell y'all that I got a hold of Akira, and he said that once we get close enough to Pikes Peak he can just pick us up."

"Why do we have to be close to Pikes?" I asked.

"Uh, Akira doesn't leave the mountain often. So he'd probably get lost otherwise." She winked. "All right," she concluded, "team meeting over."

She put her fist in the middle of our tiny circle; Andrew and I joined her, all of our knuckles touching.

Nixie seemed unsure of what we were doing so I grabbed her hand and said, "Just put your fist in like this," I showed her, "and when Fauna says 'break' you raise your arm and open your hand; got it?"

"I think so."

When she still looked confused I just shrugged and said, "It's just a thing we 30th century folks do."

"Ready?" Fauna said, "Break!" We all put our fists together then raised our hands over our heads opening them.

We all got up after that, and Fauna and Andrew took the lead while Nixie and I lagged along behind.

After a few moments Nixie said, "Thank you for telling me what to do, you'll have to teach me some more of your '30th century ways' sometime."

"Sure thing," I said, "on one condition though."

"What's that?"

"You teach me the '18th century way' in turn."

"Of course."

We walked on in silence for a ways, and I got to thinking about Pax and Belluma.

They had already been 'a part of my life' before today, and I had never even known it. What else could there possibly be that I didn't know?

I sighed, completely frazzled. I was probably ready to fray away like an old rug.

"Are you alright?" Nixie questioned me. "You seem down."

"I'm fine, it's just I feel so sorry for Pax and Belluma. They're trapped and probably going to be 'punished' for letting us escape. And if he finds out they helped us... Who knows what he'll do then."

"Kieth, you can't let this thought worry you. As I told Kavi long ago, you can't let the past bother you because what's done is done and there is no changing that. But instead look to the future with the hope that things will get better."

I stopped walking, I didn't know how to reply to her and when I didn't say anything she said, "And I now realize that this advice probably does not help one who can see the future. I'm sorry Nevio."

Hearing that name made my ears want to scream out in pain but at the moment I was not worried about the name or the advice, I had another thing going through my head, and I was almost scared to ask her about it. After a moment I finally was able to form the words I needed to ask, "Nixie, do you, ahem, still see me as Kavi?"

She blushed at my words, "Not with those yellow streaks in your hair or your green eyes. But in every other way you are his spitting image."

I still did not know whether that was a good thing or a bad thing. I let the matter die right there as we had to somewhat catch up to Fauna and Andrew and then after we caught up some Nixie stayed ahead of me so we couldn't talk easily, this was kinda disappointing, cause I liked talking to her. She was almost like another Kit but different...

...In a good way.

Chapter 23
Bionans

I knew it was going to happen even before it did.

I fell to my knees, my whole body writhing in pain. It was like my head was exploding and on fire, and filled with a thousand poking needles, all at the same time. The world seemed to spin and turn inside out before me. This was a thousand times worse than even my worst headaches.

I let loose a scream. I would normally never do this when I was in pain, I would always shut my mouth, and tolerate it. But this pain was like none I had ever felt before. It seemed like every point of my body, both inside and outside, was being poked with a million degree needle

"Kieth? What's wrong?" Nixie came over to where I lay helpless on the ground.

I couldn't answer. My only thoughts were pain, on getting rid of it, and making it stop, obliterating it, before it obliterated me.

Getting no answer from me, she called out to Fauna and Andrew, who had gotten pretty far ahead of us again,

"Fauna, something's wrong with Kieth!" She looked so worried as she watched me, while she waited for Fauna, who came running at once.

"Kieth? Kieth? What's wrong?" I flinched as she touched me; everything was pain.

"Can you hear me? Kieth!" I couldn't respond, it took all my willpower to not scream anymore.

A sudden image replaced that of Nixie, Fauna, and Andrew, and I then realized what was happening to me. I reached for the nape of my neck and only spoke one word before I blacked-out, "Bionans."

****

"How is he?"

"Same." There was a pause.

"I can't believe this is happening. What if he never wakes?"

"You can't say that! Akira's done what he can, and all we can do is pray, and wait."

The voices I was hearing were that of Nixie and Fauna. I would've said something, or moved, or something if I could, but all my limbs felt overly heavy, and every moment or so a pain jolted through each one. Nothing seemed to work but my hearing; I couldn't even open my eyes.

What had happened to me?

The thoughts were slow in coming, but eventually I remembered what had happened after escaping from the supermarket. I had passed out, but why?

Oh, right... Bionans... but what had they done to me, and why?

So many questions; too little answers. That, and my head was processing things slower than normal.

After what seemed like hours and hours of falling in and out of conscience, I was finally able to open my eyes.

At first I didn't see much at all, but then my eyes adjusted to the dimly lit room. I saw that I was in a small white room, on a hospital-like bed, and there were medical supplies all over.

Where was I?

Nixie was sitting in a chair that sat along the wall. Her head was in her hand, her eyes were closed, and she was sound asleep.

I gave a small smile as I saw Blanket lying next to me on the bed; she was asleep too. It must've been early morning, or something, since they were both asleep.

I slowly took my hand and lay it on Blanket's head petting her soft white fur. As soon as I touched her she opened her green eyes, looking at me with disbelief. She got up and hopped off the bed, and in a moment Fauna was standing over me, tears in her eyes.

"You're awake!" she said so loudly she woke the sleeping Nixie.

"Huh?" Nixie mumbled as she opened her eyes.

Fauna turned around and grabbed her hands. "Kieth's awake!" she said excitedly.

Nixie perked up and looked at me with her ice blue eyes, her hair was in a messy side braid, but it still looked good.

She smiled. "How are you feeling?"

I meant to say, 'I don't know' but it came out

more like, "I uh-o."

My voice was weak from little use, so I cleared my throat and tried again, but it was still soft, weak, and slow.

"I don't know," I repeated. "Tell me what happened, before my eyes become too heavy and I pass out again."

"Again?" Nixie asked, "What do you mean 'again'? You were awake before now?"

"Sorta... I mean... All I could do was hear things, nothing else." I rubbed my eyes,

"Augh, I feel like I've been run over by a car. Explain what happened please."

"Well," Fauna began, "Once you passed out we were thankfully not too far from where Akira could pick us up. And when he did we immediately began to try and figure out what to do with you. You sure did scare us to death; you acted like you were having seizures. As soon as we explained what little we knew of Bionans to Akira and his sister, Liegh, they began to 'investigate' the problem. They had to work quickly though cause you were just getting weaker and weaker. They said that the Bionans were consuming all the nutrients that we were giving you. So basically the Bionans were-"

I finished her sentence getting the idea, "They were killing me... eating away my flesh from the inside out..."

"They still are..." Nixie whispered.

My eyes widened, "What?!" Those things were still inside me eating away at all that kept me alive?

"Calm down Kieth!" Fauna said quickly, "Listen to me. Akira and Liegh stopped them for the time being, they concocted a suppressant, and as of now it's working."

"Wait? Can't they just get rid of them?" I asked.

"Well, they found out that there is some kind of 'home base' or 'command center' for those things, and uh, home base is, uh-" she pointed to the back of her head, "they were going to operate but decided it was way too risky because the 'command center' is literally attached to your brain stem and in between that and your cerebellum. And to take it out they may damage your brain forever."

"Wow... That's a lot to take in."

"And that's not even the half of it." She pressed a button on a remote and a TV I hadn't noticed before now came to life blaring out its news.

"And once again," the news man was saying, "we show the video of the rogue teenage Powerful's. The ones who have kidnapped Kieth, son of Dr. Forjd."

A video replaced the face of the newsman; it was security footage from the mall. It showed us running out of the door and Nixie making paint fly from the shelves.

"Authorities have been able to identify two of the three kidnappers,"

A picture of Fauna and Andrew appeared on the screen, "Kalani Fauna Forjd, niece to Dr. Forjd, and Andrew Lugen Chursland, an accomplice of Kalani. We have eyewitnesses on the powers of Chursland,

and the unknown girl. One of the workers who was a part of the confrontation was reported to have 'no memory of the encounter' and said 'it was just like any other day'.

"But we can clearly see this worker in the video. Others said that 'as soon as the girl raised her arms the paint cans flew from their shelves splattering paint everywhere'. As of now authorities have no tips of their whereabouts having found their stolen car at the bottom of a cliff. US president, River Gale, has issued a statement that everyone be on alert saying that 'the Powerfuls can be dangerous...' and in the words of Dr. Forjd..."

It went to some video of him where he said, "I just want my son back."

"We will update on the situation right after the weat-"

Fauna turned it off, "That's all they've been playing on the news channels since we got here."

"How can people be believing this stuff? I mean to me Powerfuls were only beings from a child's book before I met you."

"I'm sure some people believe it's just all some Hollywood hoax but most people will believe anything that's on the news nowadays."

All of a sudden my stomach growled embarrassingly loud.

"Gosh I don't think I've ever been this hungry. Exactly how long was I out?"

"About a week." Nixie said.

"Seriously?"

"Yeah," Fauna said, "and you can't have any food until Liegh says so. She's kinda the doctor around here."

"And when do I get to meet Liegh and Akira?"

"In the morning when everyone is actually awake. It's like two in the morning, way past my bed time." She faked a yawn. "And you should rest some more you look exhausted."

I yawned for real, "Yeah, if I can after all this devastating news." Despite what I said my eyes began to grow heavy.

Next thing I know I'm waking up to a room full of people, two of them I didn't recognize, a young man and woman.

They all had their eyes on the news, which was basically saying the same as it had last night. The young man (which I only assumed could be Akira) had his arm around Fauna's shoulders. I sat up so I could see everyone better.

Nixie was the first to see that I was awake and that I was watching them all.

She smiled, "Good morning."

I smiled back, "Morning." All eyes were on me now. I didn't know what to say or do.

"Kieth!" Fauna said, "meet Akira, and his sister Liegh."

"Nice to officially meet you, Kieth." said Liegh.

"Feelings mutual," I said weakly. I was still awfully tired. I expected greetings from Akira now but he said nothing, he only looked at Fauna for a moment then they both looked back at me.

"Akira has another way of speaking but he would like your permission for the sensation may feel intruding at first," Fauna said.

I didn't totally get what she was saying but I nodded in agreement.

As soon as I did I put my hand on my head. It didn't hurt it just felt... odd. Then the weirdest thing happened, a voice spoke to me.

It said, *'It's an honor to meet you Kieth. I am Akira. My tongue deceives me so I speak like this instead... I hope you do not mind. My sister, and I have heard much about you.'*

"Whoa," the sensation lessened, I let my hand fall back onto the bed. I looked at Akira then at Fauna.

"You sure do leave out a lot of details when speaking of things."

'I agree,' Akira said. *'She leaves out plenty of details indeed.'*

He gave her a good playful stare. I looked at Akira again. There was something vaguely familiar about him.

"You remind me of someone." I said slowly, "Someone I met not too long ago... At..." It took me a moment but then I remembered again, "...at my test in May! You were the first person to state his name. Mr. Baxon? But you look different... younger? And you could speak? .... I'm confused now."

Fauna crossed her arms, "Looks like I'm not the

only one leaving out details... what were you doing?!"

He crossed his arms too and addressed us both. *'My last name is Baxon, the reason I looked older in May was because of one of my inventions, and I was there keeping an eye on you, Fauna. Also...'* he cleared his throat. "I did not... Say, I... could not... speak."

His real voice was quiet, slurred, and very slow; his mental voice continued in my head, *'I just prefer using my Power instead.'*

"I'm sorry I didn't mean to offend-"

'You didn't,' he said, *'I get that a lot; believe me.'*

A shiver of pain ran through my body. When it was gone it left me slumped against the pillows, heart racing like I had just run a marathon.

Liegh noticed the sudden change in my health, and came over and took my pulse.

"They're acting up again," she said.

"What do you mean?" I asked breathing hard. My lungs were trying to catch up to my heart.

"It means you need more medicine." She reached over, grabbed a syringe, and stuck it in my arm. Almost instantly my heart stopped racing and my breathing slowed.

"Any better?" she asked a moment later as she grabbed another syringe.

"Yeah much," I said as she went over to Fauna, who was sitting in a chair now, and gave her the medicine in the syringe.

"You too?" I asked surprised.

"Yeah," she confessed. "But not as bad as you."

"Andrew?"

"He didn't dare touch me." He smiled. "Since every time he did he'd end up untying me."

I spoke to Fauna again, "Why didn't you tell me?"

"Because you haven't even been awake for a day yet and there was more important things to tell you. Besides my 'Bionans' can't get used to the fact that I change form every now and then and we believe they are more focused on that then on 'eating away my body'..."

My mind went into thinking mode, "Okay, why would he want to 'destroy' us or whatever... I mean, I thought he wanted us alive..."

Nixie spoke up, "We have been thinking that same thing Kieth, and Akira has a theory."

Akira's voice came back to my head, the feeling was almost like a thought that was being formed but it wasn't mine, *'Yes, well we believe that Dr. Forjds motive for using his Bionans against you both was to lure you back to him. He probably figured that we wouldn't be able to do anything and would come back to him for help. But how could he have known that we had a Powerful doctor in our midst.'* He smiled at his sister.

"But the only thing is," Liegh continued, "that we cannot kill the Bionans because they are in the most dangerous operating area ever. Your Bionans have apparently had a much longer time to develop and have therefore, in a way, merged with you.

Whereas Fauna has only had hers for a few months and a safe damage free operation is possible, hard but possible. We plan to operate in a few days."

"Operate?" I felt like I was in a room far away... everything so foreign.

"Yes, to remove the 'command center' of the Bionans. When that's gone we believe that the Bionans won't be able to function anymore."

My head began to spin. I closed my eyes. "I- I need a moment alone... to think."

There was silence, hesitation but finally they all got up and left.

Nixie was last to leave she paused at the door for a moment.

"Nixie?" I asked before she could leave.

"Yes Kieth?"

"I'm the one you were looking for... aren't I?"

She was slow in answering but finally said, "Yes, Nevio you are found."

With that she left, leaving me to my thoughts.

Truth was I couldn't think. My thoughts were all jumbled up together and that made it hard to concentrate. I was trying to think about all that was happening now but my head was trying to give me other info that made no sense.

After a minute or two I decided to sit up, cross my legs, and meditate.

I meditated on the new information, pushing out the other stuff for the time being, and after a moment I was able to welcome the information like an old memory that had just resurfaced.

~ Everything in the valley was decorated. Things went by real fast...

Soon I saw Andrew next to me. We were standing in front of Nixie who was elaborately dressed; a crown lay atop her golden hair. A flag with a circle like shape was draped on the wall behind her (I assumed this to be the Powerfuls flag).

Nixie came up to me and held out her hand, I gave her my left.

She lightly touched the inside of my arm with a wet cloth. It took all my will power not to itch my arm. She then did the same thing to Andrew.

After a few moments I noticed a mark, very similar to Fauna and Nixies, appear where the cloth had touched. It was silver.

When Nixie saw this she had us both turn around and face an eager crowd.

"Please welcome to our people, Nevio 'Dreamer of the Future', and Lugen 'The False Tongue'!"

The crowd cheered in response while waving around tiny replicas of the flag that was behind Nixie.

The scene changed. I could tell it was later that day. I was standing with a very nervous Fauna.

She was dressed in a beautiful white gown, her now red hair in a braid down her back. "Ready?" I asked.

"No..." she said as we walked arm in arm down an aisle full of people on either side. At the end of the aisle I handed her off to Akira and stood there as they made their vows to each other.

At the end of their 'I-do's' fireworks went off in the sky. It was twelve O'clock midnight of the New Year.

We all went our separate ways, some to an after party for the newlyweds; others to go home to celebrate the New Year.

I followed Nixie, Fauna, Andrew, and Akira to the lake gazebo where everyone was celebrating. I did not stay long however... something was nagging at me telling me to leave.

I said my good-byes to Akira, and Andrew first. Then came Fauna.

She cried as I hugged her and said good-bye. She knew the real reason I was leaving.

"Are you sure you have to go?" she sobbed.

"Yes, I'm sorry." Was all I could manage to say. I handed her a note, "Could you please make sure this gets to Nixie?"

"You're not going to tell her yourself?" she asked surprised.

"I don't think I could bring myself to do it..." I paused, "just please get it to her?"

"Of course!" she said as I began to leave. "Just be safe, okay?"

"I will." I left her there, tears still in her green eyes.

I went to my little room, changed, and then gathered my already ready backpack. From there I walked to the edge of the lake.

Turning around, I took one last look.

Getting into that little boat that would take me to the other side of the lake, away from this hidden valley of Powerfuls, away from the people whom I was endangering, was real hard.

And all I could do now, I thought as I paddled across the lake, was to go wherever my dreams took me. ~

Acknowledgments

There are many people to thank for helping me accomplish what I have done.

But first and foremost is my wonderful sister Haliegh (I'm making sure it's spelt right sis). She has been there steps one through one hundred and beyond and is most always the first one to see what I have written. Love ya Hal!

Secondly to my awesome Aunt Angie who has also been one of the first to see my writings. I always look forward to see what she thinks about this idea and that idea.

Thirdly to Greg who has helped critique my work and give me advice on writing strategies.

I would also like to thank my friend Katey who has given me many ideas and support.

Thanks a lot to my Mom, Dad, and brother who have decided to finally read my book when it's published. Love you guys!

Also thank you to Grace for drawing me the symbol on the front cover and to my Grandparents who have always asked for more! (I put the dragon reference in there just for you Papa!)

"For I know the plans I have for you... Plans to give you a hope and a future."
Jeremiah 29:11

~To God be the Glory! Great things He is Doing~